WOLF PROTECTOR
FEDERAL PARANORMAL UNIT

BOOK ONE

NEW YORK TIMES and USA TODAY
BESTSELLING AUTHOR

MILLY TAIDEN

EBooks are not transferable. They cannot be sold, shared, or given away. The unauthorized reproduction or distribution of this copyrighted work is a crime punishable by law. No part of this book may be scanned, uploaded to or downloaded from file sharing sites, or distributed in any other way via the Internet or any other means, electronic or print, without the publisher's permission. Criminal copyright infringement, including infringement without monetary gain, is investigated by the FBI and is punishable by up to 5 years in federal prison and a fine of $250,000 (http://www.fbi.gov/ipr/).

This book is a work of fiction. The names, characters, places, and incidents are fictitious or have been used fictitiously, and are not to be construed as real in any way. Any resemblance to persons, living or dead, actual events, locales, or organizations is entirely coincidental.

Wolf Protector
Copyright © 2013 by Milly Taiden

Published By
Latin Goddess Press
New York, NY 10456
http://millytaiden.com

Edited by Dee Carrell
Cover by Willsin Rowe
Formatted by AG Formatting

All Rights Are Reserved.

Property of Milly Taiden March 2013

WOLF PROTECTOR

A woman with a secret... The Federal Paranormal Unit is an elite squad of supernaturals dedicated to solving missing persons cases. Erica's gift allows her a special connection with the crime, but it comes at a deep personal cost... Until now, she's kept her gift a secret, even from the other members of the team. But this case will throw her together with Agent Trent Buchanan. He's the object of her secret desires, but he's also a cocky womanizer. She'd rather swim in shark-infested waters with a paper cut than admit she has feelings for him.

A man with one desire... Wolf Shifter Trent wants Erica more than he's ever wanted any woman. He's spent years patiently waiting for her to admit that she wants him too. Working one-on-one in a race to find a serial killer, Trent's patience and Erica's resolve wear thin. When Trent discovers the truth about Erica, will he accept her for who she is? And can he protect her from the horrors that her gift brings?

A case that pushes them to the edge... Erica will have to risk it all if she wants to stop the killer, and when she does, Trent may have to put his own life on the line to make sure his mate is protected...

To all the wonderful people who made this book possible. A special thank you to each of the following:

Thank you for all your support and help.

To all my readers: I hope you enjoy Trent and Erica's story

ONE

"Brock, he's doing it again!" Erica glared at the Casanova walking beside her, hating how good he looked in his black T-shirt and ass-hugging jeans. Trent Buchanan. He was her daily temptation and ultimate fantasy. And she'd rather wax her nipples in public than admit it to him. Butterflies swarmed her stomach, twisting and twirling her into one giant, aroused mess.

"What's Buchanan done this time, Villa?" Brock, their team leader, asked without looking up from the papers on his desk.

"He's staring at me." She growled and dropped in one of the empty chairs, huffing out a breath.

Buchanan, The Bastard, as she liked to refer to his cute ass, grinned at her. His full, sexy lips caught her immediate attention. "Excuse me, I can't help it if it's a beautiful day, and I'm glad it's Friday. You're a grump, Villa."

It was so unfair that she had to keep pushing him away when her body wanted to curl around his big frame. But if she ever did that she'd turn into another Trent groupie, and that was not her thing. She'd seen the other women in the department walk after him, ogling and almost drooling, as if he were the lead singer in a rock band. *Pathetic*.

Buchanan folded his arms over his massive chest. Erica's entire body throbbed every time she looked at him. She drank in the inciting vision and argued with her lust for dominance. Disgusted with her body's responses, she glared at him again. Her eyes strayed to the scar on his upper lip. She gulped and curled her fingers into her palms, digging her nails deep. Whenever she glanced at the tiny scar, she wanted to nibble and run her tongue over it. It was driving her insane. Thankfully he couldn't read her mind, or he'd be having a hell of a time making fun of her tough talk.

"Villa, just look at me." He opened his muscled arms wide and did a full circle for her. Once he was facing her again, he leaned on the wall. He winked at her. "If you didn't have a stick the size of Texas up your ass, you'd realize what a catch I am."

"Ouch." Jane Donovan, the youngest member in their team exclaimed as she entered the office. "You are looking to get your little boy parts cut off when you least expect it, Buchanan."

Donovan sat next to Erica and played with her phone, or what appeared to be a phone. She was a systems expert and always had some strange gadget in her hands.

Erica peeked at Buchanan again and frowned. It wasn't smart to let him get the best of her, she knew that, but something about him made her speak without thinking.

Buchanan grinned, lifted a hand to his lips, and blew her an air kiss. "Villa knows she wants me. If she would stop fighting her instincts we'd have moved past this awkward foreplay."

And that was the reason Erica would rather swim in shark-infested waters with a paper cut than admit her attraction to the six-foot-two wall of sexy muscle. Even if her body was strung so tight she thought she'd soon burst a blood vessel, she would not admit to her growing desire for Buchanan.

"Settle down. Where the hell is Ramirez?"

Brock asked, finally looking up at the three of them.

"Probably getting some in the men's room." Donovan muttered under her breath.

Erica choked on a giggle. They were so going to get written up. Brock didn't allow that kind of talk around the building, ever. It was hard enough that they were held to higher standards than the other teams. The senior directors expected miracles from them. Erica was lucky Brock took the brunt of the stress from his superiors.

Buchanan groaned. "Am I missing out on something that awesome? Because I had no idea women were doing that in the men's room."

Erica's smile fell from her lips. He continued to grin at her. "Don't worry, Villa. I'm all yours whenever you want me. Just say the word."

"I said settle down," Brock ordered again. "This is not the time or place for this type of behavior. You know we have a strict code of conduct here."

Did Buchanan ever not think of sex? Probably not. Shit, even she had a hard time keeping her thoughts away from sex whenever he was around.

Before she got the chance to give him a sarcastic response, Tony Ramirez strolled in, an easy smile over his wide lips. He was a specimen of male perfection, able to make the strongest of women pant. Of course, he also had an ego the size of Alaska. But as much as she'd tried, her panties just didn't go into a desperate twist with Ramirez. Oh but with Trent…er Buchanan, her body buzzed in awareness the moment he swaggered into the room with her.

"I'm here. Sorry, I was caught up." Ramirez's tone dripped with innuendo.

"Oh, brother." Donovan's complaint was loud. "Are we here for another lesson on who can get more? Ramirez versus Buchanan? Because, I gotta say, I have better things to do than figure that one out. As far as I'm concerned the women both of these dumbasses get don't count. They're all easy."

"Hey!" Both men complained at once.

Brock's patience snapped. "Enough!" His voice thundered in the office, making the entire team go silent. "We are not here for a competition on who has the biggest anything, so put your rulers away and pay attention. I don't want to write anyone up on misconduct, so please, shut your mouths before I'm forced to." He took a deep breath and rubbed his fingers over his eyes before looking up. His gaze pierced each of them as it traveled the room. "Let's get to what you're here for. You all have a new assignment."

He handed each of the team members a file. When Erica opened the folder, her heartbeat slowed to a thudding crawl. She dropped the file on her lap and stared. A photo of a woman's naked, lifeless body sat at the top of the paperwork.

"That is Lisa Summers. Age: Nineteen. She was a student at a large state college in upstate New York. She was walking home after her last class and never made it back to her apartment."

Erica studied the photo and placed her hands on the chair's metal armrests. She knew if she touched the photo she would not like what she saw. The woman's pale flesh was marred with bruising, cuts, and burns. A sick knot settled in Erica's throat, growing with every second she stared at the body. Instant grief for the dead girl filled her. She lifted her gaze from the file and found Brock watching her. Only he knew of her ability.

Everyone else thought she did some kind of profiling. The truth was she got glimpses of people's highest energy level moments by touching something of theirs, and that included photos of their deceased bodies. A photo could capture a small amount of a person's energy. Captured energy, even the small bits caught in pictures, was enough to help her connect with the victim. "Why are we seeing a photo of a dead woman instead of a missing one?" Erica asked.

Brock shifted, glancing from one person to the next until his gaze landed back on Erica. She knew whatever he said next was directed just to her.

"Lisa isn't victim number one. She's the first one found. According to the medical examiner, she was killed forty-eight hours ago. Her body was placed in an alley."

The nervous shaking of Ramirez's legs never slowed as he crossed and uncrossed them. "Do you think it's a ritual killing? Or something like an angry ex-boyfriend?"

Erica hated to think there were more young women out there being tortured to death. Tearing her sight from the horrific image of the dead body, she gulped, eyeing everyone in the office. Donovan scribbled furiously. Paper scrunched under her hands as she flicked from one page to the next, her red hair brushing her cheek and sliding forward when she lowered her face toward the notepad. Ramirez frowned, as if trying to solve the puzzle himself while staring at the photo. Buchanan's gaze connected with Erica's. Her heart flipped at his intense look. She gripped the chair, keeping herself from squirming in her seat.

"I don't know, but we don't think so." Brock's voice jerked her back to reality. Against her will, she broke contact with Buchanan's dark stare and faced Brock.

Taking a slow breath, she glanced down at the photo again. "Not a ritual... This was a crime of revenge." She swiped her tongue over her bottom lip, thinking of reasons, reasons why anyone would be battered and beaten the way Lisa Summers had been, and continued to contemplate the photo. "I'm almost inclined to say passion, but I can see a savagery to this scene I rarely encounter."

"So you don't think it's a serial?" Buchanan's breath tickled the side of her neck. He'd moved closer to her seat and peered at the file over her shoulder. He had his own, but he chose to look at hers instead.

She tried not to shudder, but listening to the raspy tone gave her goose bumps. "I didn't say that. What I'm saying is whoever killed her had a reason. One we have to discover as soon as possible." Her stomach churned at what she'd need to do. Tension slid down her spine, expanding with every inch it traveled. She glanced at Brock. "I need to see the body."

Brock slapped his hands down on the file. The loud thump caught everyone off guard and made Donovan jump in her seat with a gasp. "All right. We're going to do something different this time." He stared at Erica. "I know that I have usually teamed up with Villa, but this time I need to stay here. The mayor has scheduled multiple meetings, and our department head wants me there. I tried to get out of it, but it was a no-go."

His words ratcheted up the anxiety inside her, until it was hard for her to hear through her wall of unease.

What did that mean for her?

"I'm going to need you, Villa, Ramirez, and Buchanan, to head up there first. The three of you are going to work this case, ASAP. Gather your gear, and be ready to stay a while. I'm sure you all know what this crime looks like, and I'm not waiting around to see where it goes. Apparently a couple of senators have daughters up there, and they want this resolved immediately."

Buchanan shifted away from Erica's shoulder to stand upright. She couldn't stop herself; she peeked up. She instantly missed his body heat, the scent of his musky cologne, and his warm breath by her ear. They had all mixed together to make her feel that much more wound up. "You said she wasn't victim number one."

Brock rubbed a hand over the back of his neck, his forehead creased with doubt. "I don't think she is. Lisa had been missing for a week, but another student went missing before her. Gina Torres disappeared two weeks ago. There's no trace of her anywhere."

Donovan, who had been taking notes, stopped and looked up, her green eyes filled with curiosity. "How do we know *she's* victim number one?"

Brock shrugged. Focusing on Erica, he gave a slight shake of his head. "We don't know. In fact, we know very little. It's your job to find out what happened to her. See what you discover. I want you to move quickly. I don't want a string of dead college girls making the national papers." His brows dipped low in a solemn frown. "Nichol's in charge while you're up there. Donovan and I will look into things from here. If there is any news on Torres or any other new victims, we'll head your way." He shut the file with a slam. "Go, find what you can, and let's get some answers."

She stood to go, but Brock shook his head.

"Villa, I need to discuss some things with you for a moment."

Buchanan's dark eyes locked on her, again. A measure of reassurance and something else were visible in his steady gaze. The urge to fidget and turn away coursed through her. She hated when he stared at her like that. She could handle his silly quips and sexual innuendos, but once he regarded her like he cared, it scared the crap out of her.

"Sure thing."

She waited. Increasing apprehension gathered at the thought of the upcoming trip. The others marched out in single file. Ramirez, the last one to step out, shut the door behind him. Taking her seat again, she opened the manila folder on her lap. It took a minute to urge her mind to focus. Looking at the photo was like having hot coals burned into her eye sockets. She could visualize how the woman got her injuries from a hundred different angles and viewpoints. Because Erica connected with the victim's energy, the clearest flashes were of moments where the victim's energy spiked. Usually that meant a moment of fear, or worse, the moment of death. When she glanced up, Brock was observing her. Unease curled into a jagged ball inside her.

"Brock?"

He sighed as he dropped into the seat next to her. "Villa, I know I'm the only person you work with. But we're a team, and I need you to be able to work alone with the rest of them. It's time to trust that we all have your back. This unit—our unit—is not normal. We all know that. Each of you has a particular trait that makes you necessary to the team. Yours is a little different than the others, but it is one of the most important. Because of this, I need you to take charge in this case."

This was major for her. She didn't trust anyone on a good day. Anxiety spread through her limbs in a cold sweep that made her shudder. Security dictated none of them share their gifts with each other. In case of someone leaving or getting captured, no vital information would be lost. But what if the others realized what she did? What she was?

"I want you to be very careful with this. There is something about this case that doesn't sit right with me. This body, it wasn't just displayed. It was grandstanded. Whoever killed her wanted us to find her."

She regarded Brock, the only person who had not let her down so far. She nodded. It might be scary, or more like frickin' terrifying, but she'd work with the others—without him. Although she didn't want to admit it, the thought of working one-on-one with Buchanan sent a hot shiver up her spine, thawing some of the anxiety a new case brought. She glanced down at the photo, all the while keeping her hands from touching the glossy paper. Because reality was, she wanted to put off the nightmares of the woman's last, painful seconds for as long as possible.

"Do you know anything about her? Her family or friends? Anyone who might have had it in for her?" She stared at the positioning of the body, made mental notes, and visually recorded several things that made her breath hitch. The girl was definitely on display.

Whoever killed her wanted her found in the way she'd been placed: spread-eagle with her arms open to her sides, allowing for everyone who looked to see the jagged wounds from the knife cuts on her stomach. She wasn't a small woman, so whoever moved her around had to have the muscle to do so. A fuzzy image of the killer started to form.

Brock shook his head. "No. That's one of the things you guys have to look into. The town she was murdered in is small, and their police force needs the extra help. This is the first murder they've seen in a long time. She was attending the university, but her body was found in a smaller township close to where she lived."

Erica nodded. Brock watched her with the same concern and scrutiny he showed during every investigation. It was his big-brother attitude. "Do you think you can do this?" he asked. "You'll be seeing more when you get to her house."

She took a deep breath and let it out gradually, forcing her thoughts to stop jumping around.

"Will you be able to work with Buchanan? I'm worried about you. I need to know you can work this case. Can you handle working one-on-one with him?"

This was new, and she and Trent…Buchanan were going to be working long hours alone.

Could she handle it? Probably not, but she'd never admit to that. No matter how hard it was, she never backed out of a new case. "Yes, I know. I can handle it. I'll get whoever did this. I will do whatever I have to in order to solve this and find out who killed Lisa."

Brock grabbed her forearm and gave her a quick squeeze. "Don't touch anything unless you absolutely have to."

His demand sounded more like a request. He was the only person that knew how hard it was for her, how much she struggled with each case. To see the things she saw of the victims inside her mind. She saw them all being held captive, tortured, and killed. And that could turn any day into a living hell for her.

All she visualized for months was blurred bits of the victims' last moments. Sometimes, she'd get lucky and actually *see*. "I know that for you to get a glimpse of something—anything—helpful is the ultimate payoff. But there have been too many times when you don't get anything useful, only the bad. I want you to try to focus on what you see with your eyes, what your instinct tells you, what the people say, and what you can uncover without your extra sensory sight."

She frowned. "You know that the best images I get are from touching. I won't have the same clear view after that first connection. Initial contact with something belonging to the victim is the biggest break we can get. Things become hazy, unfocused, and mangled after that. I will do my best, but if I have to touch...I will."

Shutting the manila folder, and with it the torturous vision of the woman's corpse, she got up to go. At the same time, Brock stood, towering over her. He placed a hand on her shoulder. "No heroics, Erica. I need you mentally and emotionally stable to work this case. Don't overdo it. Don't touch things if you're not ready to see."

"I'll be fine. Stop worrying, Brock." She smiled, her vision straying outside past the glass door. Buchanan sat on the edge of Donovan's desk. The way he looked at her, so possessive and dark, fired more than her interest. If she wasn't careful this case would turn into her biggest fight against her body and its desires.

Brock leaned down by her ear, and her heart leapt when Buchanan clenched his jaw. "Don't let him get the best of you. He's a good guy, but if you need me to handle him just let me know."

She knew how intimate the moment appeared to Buchanan and added her own bit of fire into the mix by smiling at Brock. "Don't worry, I can handle him."

She left Brock's office a mass of ne stress had just gone from hair-fal' won't-be-getting-any-sleep level in the blink of an eye.

"Okay, so explain to me again where we're going first?" Ramirez's voice floated from the backseat of the Jeep.

Erica twisted her long hair into a sloppy bun at the top of her head and groaned. God, the humidity up here was horrible. And she probably looked like Medusa. She grabbed a water bottle from the cup holder and took a long gulp. It was the end of July, and a heat wave had taken over the northeast. Her tank top was stuck uncomfortably to her back. Heat and humidity were not her friends. Not to mention the mosquitoes. Already they'd encountered a large number of the annoying little bugs. She hated bugs. She hated anything that crawled and had more than two feet, or worse, no feet. She shuddered just visualizing them.

"To see the body," Buchanan replied. "Per Brock's orders that's stop number one."

Erica peeked at Buchanan's smiling profile from behind her sunglasses. All dressed in black, he looked like a super hot Navy Seal. The T-shirt did nothing to cover the bulging muscles that rippled whenever he gripped the wheel. His short, spiky hair and five o'clock shadow made him look oh-so fine. And the reflective sunglasses added to his sexy, bad-boy allure. Goddamn it, she needed to get laid! Pronto, or she'd start seeing Buchanan as more than a Casanova and more like a possible candidate to end her sexual hiatus.

Her mind started to wander. What was it that made Buchanan special to their team? He did have a military background, but there was a restrained wildness about him that made her keep him at a distance. Not because she couldn't handle it, but because she knew that she'd probably enjoy it way too much. It was dangerous for her emotions and for her hormones. He was hot, and she could only fight them for so long. She wondered what he was. Was he a warlock? An empath? Or maybe he had some other ability… She'd always worked with Brock one-on-one, so she hadn't seen Buchanan in action before now.

Buchanan turned his face toward her and smiled the sexy smile that made her entire body throb. It made her want to lick and suck at the little scar on his lip.

"Like what you see, Villa? I can give you a private show later. Just you and me, baby." His deep voice promised so much pleasure that it took a moment for her brain to process the actual words.

She blinked. He'd caught her staring at him. Of all the stupid things for her to do. "Actually, I was wondering if it was possible for you to actually have a brain inside that skull. You know what they say; the bigger the brawn, the smaller the brain."

He smiled, unperturbed. "Trust me, Villa. My brain is big enough to amaze any woman who sees it. In fact, the last time one saw it she called me a god."

The tone of his voice sounded deeper than before. She was practically panting over his rough timbre. It took her a second to realize what he'd said. Pangs of jealousy hit her low in the gut. She lost her smile at the thought of him with another woman and turned away. Her mind was a muddled mess over how much she hated the thought of him with someone else. She'd let her guard down too much with him, and it surprised her. Looking out her window, she focused on the passing trees. "Ramirez, what do we know about our victim?"

Along with the hum of the air conditioner, Ramirez's soft Latin voice filled the inside of the Jeep. "Lisa Summers was a freshman at Ithaca. She lived in a small town not far from the school. Her family resides in New York City. She was from a very sheltered home and was not even allowed to have a sleepover. Apparently it took her almost a year to convince her parents to let her go away to school. She'd wanted overseas. They wanted down the street. Both compromised with out of town but same state."

Erica nodded absently. "What about boyfriends? Friends? Exes?"

"No current boyfriends. She did have a lot of friends. She was a very popular girl and went out a lot. I guess she decided that her sheltered lifestyle was over the minute she left home."

Erica shook her head. The poor girl hadn't realized that danger could also lurk in this quiet, small town. "Have the friends been interviewed by the police? Do they know anything useful to help give us a clue where to look first?"

"Some of her friends have been. It seems most of the kids have rich parents, and as soon as word got out, no one wanted to say any more without a lawyer present."

She cursed under her breath. "Do we at least have any idea who was the last person to see her alive?"

"Yes. It was her best friend, Gia Matthews. She said they had parted ways after their last class. Normally they would head home together, since they lived in the same building, but the friend had a date and Lisa went home on her own. Apparently, Lisa didn't have any plans to go out that evening and was planning to study for an upcoming exam."

Erica watched as they turned onto a main street. The trees along the street gave way to some shops, a post office, a couple of family restaurants, and a police station. Each one looking older than the last; the structures appeared to have been built in the earlier part of the last century. The store next to the police station had peeled paint, rusted metal bars, and windows that looked like some she'd seen on the History Channel. Buchanan stopped in front of the small police station. A lone car sat outside the square-looking building. She jumped out of the Jeep, and wiped her sweaty palms on the back of her khaki shorts.

She winced when steamy heat hit her in the face. Beads of sweat gathered on her upper lip and the back of her neck, and dripped down her temples. She strolled toward the entrance to the single-story building with a lone thought: It was absolutely necessary for her to keep her mind focused solely on the case. She scanned the outside of the building. Looking more like a general store than a secure location to question criminals, the station was small with a wide-open entrance.

Inside, she went straight up to the wooden counter, where papers and files littered the scarred old surface. Buchanan and Ramirez followed behind her. A short, pot-bellied older man with a long beard and thick mustache stood when he saw her enter. His brown uniform shirt wrinkled against his heavy frame, and his bald-head showed off his liver spots.

The old man peered at Erica from under heavy gray brows, his piercing gaze moving to Buchanan and, after a moment, finally landing on Ramirez.

"Can I help you?"

"Yes." She pulled up the ID badge that hung from her neck on a silver chain, flicked it open, displaying her photo and agency details. "I'm Agent Villa, Federal Bureau of Investigation. These are my colleagues: Agents Ramirez and Buchanan. We're here to see Lisa Summers's body, Mister…"

"Deputy Owens, Carl Owens. Welcome to Shady Oaks," he replied and shook the hand she offered. A grin spread across his wrinkled face.

"Could you please show us Ms. Summers's body, Deputy Owens?"

Deputy Owens nodded. "Yes, ma'am."

He glanced down at the counter, shuffled papers, and placed them into folders. "We've had a few out-of-town reporters wanting to see the body, so I've had to stay here and guard it until you all came along. We put it in the morgue. You'll have to forgive us, but this is the first murder in our town in over fifty years. The morgue is a really small room."

He walked to the end of the counter, opened a door, and allowed them into his side of the room. With each step he took the heavy key ring jingled, reminding Erica of a bag of coins being shaken. The three of them followed the deputy down the hall until he stopped in front of a large metal door. Cool air seeped out from underneath it.

"You're sure you want to see this ma'am? It's a mighty nasty sight."

Erica nodded. "I'm sure, Deputy Owens. Go ahead and let us inside."

He opened the door, and Erica walked into a cold, windowless storage room. It was no bigger than a twelve-foot by twelve-foot cell. As soon as she stepped inside, the stench of rotting flesh surrounded her, digging into her lungs and making her scrunch her face in distaste. In the middle of the room sat a metal table with the body, covered by a white sheet.

Buchanan strode up to the small, wheeled cart next to the body, pulled on some gloves, and opened a jar of odor-perception inhibitor. He grabbed the jar, held it away from his nose, and then he clutched a second pair of gloves, bringing both over to her. Still fighting the urge to gag, she put the gloves on and patted a finger full of the paste under her nostrils, masking some of the rotting body stench.

"Don't you need any?"

Buchanan shook his head and made a face showing his distaste. "That stuff stinks."

Her jaw dropped. "The body stinks more."

"I can handle the body."

She shrugged. With both hands to her sides, she walked up to the table where the body lay.

Ramirez dragged the sheet back. Erica's stomach clenched and she was glad she'd forgone breakfast. She swallowed, pushing down the urge to vomit. The victim, Lisa, had been strangled. She had also been stabbed, beaten, and mutilated. The word "Bitch" was carved into her stomach.

Ramirez whistled under his breath. "Jesus. Talk about anger. That is some fucked-up shit right there. That girl is way more than dead. She's an example. Somebody wanted her in pain. More pain than what I see in most victims."

Buchanan started sniffing, and Erica raised her brows.

"Are you ok?"

He sneezed. "Bleach. This body was thoroughly cleaned before it was dumped."

She inhaled, but all she got was the scent of the inhibitor under her nose. "How can you tell?"

He scrunched his nose, turned back to her, and took a step back. "Trust me, I can tell. So what's your first impression, Villa?"

"She was so young."

She said the words softly while glancing at the girl. The victim's face and body were a large map of bruises.

"The cuts on the body appear to have been made with a scalpel. I'm not sure about determining this person to be in the medical profession because the pre-mortem lines are jagged." She leaned over the body and studied the wounds with more intensity. Buchannan and Ramirez walked up and did the same. She glanced up and saw them frown, as if they were trying to figure out what she saw.

"If you look closely," she pointed a gloved finger toward some of the wounds, "you will notice that the killer started out with smooth lines, but something got the best of him. As if he wanted to hurry up and finish the cutting…"

"What? Like he was excited and wanted to see the words carved so he rushed through the job? Or like he was nervous because he was doing something he shouldn't be?" Ramirez picked up one of the surgical instruments and studied it with interest.

"I'm not sure," she whispered. She continued

to study the cuts, each one more horrific than the last. Instinct and something inside told her this wasn't going to be the only one. And she was definitely an example.

Yes, an example to others. Erica continued to stare at the body. Her attention was on the young girl's face. She moved around the table, taking in the body from a different angle. Her heart beat in loud thuds in her chest. Curling her nails into her palms, she approached her victim's face. She tuned out Ramirez and Buchanan and focused on the girl. So young. Alone. Scared.

Irritation mounted at her lack of focus. She took a deep breath and examined the girl's lifeless features. Colorful bruises marred her cheeks. He beat her because she fought. There are bruises on her knuckles. She didn't just die; she'd fought to live, and he'd enjoyed the kill. Erica closed her eyes and got a glimpse into a room. Dark. Angry. Fear crawled up her spine when a voice whispered into her ear. *"You will regret your choice."*

"Can you guys give me a moment to analyze this body? I just think better alone."

Buchanan eyed her warily while Ramirez nodded. The soft click of the door made her heartbeat accelerate. She turned in a circle to make sure she was alone.

"Ok, Lisa…"

She gulped and stared at the body. Cold shivers racked her. She hated this part but knew it was necessary. Her best and clearest images came from touching the body itself and picking up on residual energy victims left behind.

She walked around the table and stopped by Lisa's arm. Her lungs fought to get air in. She grabbed hold of Lisa's cold hand between hers and gasped.

The victim's heart-wrenching scream filled her ears. Pain, sorrow, and despair all flooded her mind. The movie-like images made her breath catch. It showed her the minute the girl had realized her plight. These were Lisa's final moments. She couldn't breathe or move. Darkness surrounded her, and the scent of wood invaded her senses. Lisa's heart beat so fast she thought she was having a panic attack.

She was in a box, a coffin. Panicked screams tore from her throat, and her hands beat at the wood. She'd been buried alive. Terror, raw and nerve-wracking, filled her mind when she realized she was going to die.

Erica jerked to the present with so much force she fell to her knees. Her body shook. She gulped, trying to catch her breath and still feeling as though she couldn't breathe. The panic Lisa had felt was still thick and heavy inside her. Tears filled her eyes. It hurt to see someone suffering the way Lisa had been.

Moments later she was standing by the body making notes. She continued to visualize how Lisa had gotten each of her wounds.

The door opened and Buchanan and Ramirez walked back inside.

"Hey, Villa. Did you forget we were out there? Damn it's hot." Ramirez wiped his brow.

She went back to studying Lisa's body. The longer she stared at the wounds, the more it hurt her to breathe.

Buchanan's voice broke through her connection. "Villa? Are you alright?"

Erica jerked sideways, until she was facing away from the girl, and gulped a breath. When she turned to face Buchanan and Ramirez, both men were watching her. She'd never been with anyone other than Brock when she connected with the victim. "Fine. I'm fine. Let's go to her apartment. We really need to get moving on this case."

Before more bodies turned up.

"You sure you're alright, Villa?" Buchanan asked once they were back inside the Jeep and headed to the victim's apartment.

She needed to think. She'd already written down the glimpse into the dark room along with the quick flash of struggle she'd seen. It wasn't enough. More information was needed in order to get a better, much more detailed description of the killer. There was only one way to achieve that.

"Buchanan, just because I saw a dead body doesn't make me a weakling. Stop looking so scared. It's not like I'm going to run to you expecting you to protect me." She batted her lashes and draped the back of her hand over her forehead with a dramatic sigh. "'Oh hold me, Trent. I'm so scared. Whatever will I do?'"

She made light of the situation, hoping he'd ignore what he'd seen.

Ramirez laughed from the backseat. Erica grinned, but when she turned to Buchanan he wasn't smiling, he was watching her intently. She turned away from him, put her sunglasses over her eyes, and fought her body's need to seek him out. The last thing she needed was for him to realize how disturbed she'd been by being near the body.

The drive to Lisa Summers's apartment complex was short. Once they arrived, Buchanan used the key the deputy had given him to gain access to the place. She didn't touch anything, knowing the result if she did. After a quick scan of the area, she noticed the place still appeared ready for Lisa to come home. The police report said everything had been left as it had been found. They'd blocked off all access into the apartment.

Sand took over her throat, clogging it and making it hard to swallow. A short-lived moment of indecision stopped her, but she steeled her spine and moved toward the bedroom. Buchanan followed her. She eyed the room with trepidation, strolled into the large space and stopped a foot away from the bed. Even though his presence soothed her nerves, she needed to be alone in the room. Before she got a chance to ask him to leave, he turned toward the door.

"Are you going to be all right in here?" He glanced around at the frilly bedding and curtains. Lisa Summers had been a girly-girl. "I'm going to check around the living area. Call if you find anything."

"I'm fine. Shut the door behind you," she ordered. The soft click of the lock let her know he'd followed her request.

Her blood froze as nerves attempted to get the better of her, but she proceeded to the bed and grabbed hold of the comforter.

TWO

Trent went through the victim's mail, wondering why there were no more persons of interest. He'd scented the place, knowing that Ramirez was doing the same. It was what they did. Shifters followed their senses, and smell was the top one.

Erica was not a shifter. And from what Brock had told him, she didn't know about shifters. But they were all aware everyone in the unit was special. Each one was just too private to share with the others. Ramirez was the only one who knew his secret. The white tiger shifter had become Ramirez's best friend years ago, but he had no clue what type of paranormal the others were. He couldn't scent anything but human in

Erica or Donovan. Brock was…different. He couldn't put his finger on what his leader was, but it was definitely not human.

A muffled sound, coming from the bedroom, made him drop the letters and frown. A second noise, which sounded like a low moan, had both him and Ramirez darting to the bedroom. Erica's cry increased in volume with each step. He growled, pulled out his gun, and he charged through the door, looking for an intruder. His first instinct had been to shift, but he didn't want to scare Erica to death.

"What the fuck? Villa?" He rushed toward her when he got no response, still searching around the room for the danger. The scent of her fear was overpowering. He didn't know what was wrong, but it was making his wolf insane to know she was hurting.

"Erica?" He stopped a few feet from her and stared. She held the comforter in a white-knuckle grip. She struggled to breathe.

"Is she all right?" Ramirez's voice deepened in readiness to shift.

"Yeah. You go back and make sure nobody comes in here. I'll take care of her." When Ramirez walked out the door, Trent frowned at Erica again. She stood completely still, the comforter in her grip. With a few steps, he closed the distance between them until he stood next to her, wincing at the anguish in her face. Her eyes were closed and tears streamed down her cheeks. She whimpered.

"Help me, please." Her voice sounded clogged with pain and panic. Her distress was so genuine; it made the hairs on his arms rise. Agony, fear, and desperation bled through her plea for help. His wolf pushed at the skin cage, wanting out. His need to protect Erica became his sole focus.

Concerned only for her safety, he grabbed her by the arms, hauled her away from the bed and the comforter, and hugged her tightly. When she started gulping air, he drew away and scanned her face and eyes. She appeared to be in a trance, her eyes cloudy and unfocused.

It scared the shit out of him.

"Erica? Erica!" The shift rushed him, and it was hell reining back his animal. He shook her a couple times until she blinked. Her glassy eyes concentrated on him.

Her breathing slowly returned to normal. "Trent?" The moment he opened his mouth to answer, her caramel skin paled even further and her eyes rolled backward. Her body slumped forward, right into his arms.

Whatever the hell was wrong with Erica, he wasn't going to leave her in the bedroom that had affected her so strongly. It was clear she sensed things. No wonder Brock was always so protective of her. He picked her up and marched toward the front entrance. When he got to the living room, Ramirez was waiting by the door.

Ramirez frowned at Erica's limp body. "What happened?"

Trent walked out the door. He hated how a gray color had overtaken her healthy bronzed skin tone, knowing Ramirez would follow behind. "I don't know, but something made her freak the fuck out."

"I'll keep looking to see if I find anything here. I'll be down in a few minutes." Ramirez yelled to Trent.

Trent was beyond pissed; he wanted to break something. His wolf wanted to get out and kill. Seeing Erica look so helpless had pushed him to act. Something inside him had snapped when he'd seen his little she-devil in so much pain. It was one thing to watch her tell him off with her cheeky grin. But no matter how strong she was, and he knew she was very strong to be able to work with their team; he couldn't stand by and do nothing when she was clearly suffering.

He sat in the back of the Jeep with her in his arms at the moment his sharp-tongued harpy was too pale, and it scared him. Possession heated his blood.

The moment he'd met her he'd known she was his mate. Her scent had pulled him immediately, but the way she fought her attraction to him pushed him away. He wanted her. It sucked big-time that she, the one woman he would give everything up for, didn't pay him any serious attention. No matter what he tried, she was oblivious to his charm.

Well, not entirely. He smelled her desire for his body, but that wasn't new. He wanted her to get to know him, to want him. Erica was his mate. He knew eventually she'd give him a chance. He was nothing if not persistent.

Caressing her smooth cheek, he called out to her. "Erica? Wake up, Erica."

Her eyes jerked opened, and she blinked. "What do you think you're doing?"

"Holding you." Relief that she was speaking so clearly made his breath trip in his chest.

She sat up in his lap and wiggled to get off. The move made him hard as a rock in a second. He was such a sick bastard. Erica had just suffered some kind of nervous faint, and here he was ready to spread her thighs open and slide into her without a second's hesitation.

"I need a phone," she demanded. "Right now." Her voice sounded wobbly as she peered around the inside of the Jeep.

He was about to tell her to take it easy when she reached to the front cup holder and made a quick grab for her cell phone. She sat back down next to him. A moment later, she pressed a few buttons with shaky fingers, put the phone to her ear, and turned her face away from him to stare out the windshield.

"It's Villa. We went to Lisa Summers's apartment. My first impression is that she didn't get a chance to see her killer. She was held inside a box, underground, before he finally pulled her out and strangled her. The wounds, the cuts were made while she was alive. She was able to feel it. She tried to fight, but she'd been drugged." She bit her lip, rubbing her right temple with her hand.

"I think that allowed him to bury her alive, which was his way of teaching her a lesson." She sat there unmoving, her posture rigid, and listened to her phone. "No. We're looking for someone young, strong, and angry. Yes, we'll go through the friends and any males she had contact with."

She glanced at Trent and quickly looked away.

Something strange was going on. He could hear the other side of the conversation. Brock kept asking her how she was feeling, but she didn't answer him. Anger and concern rolled through him in equal measures. This wasn't his little hellcat, not at all. What had happened? Why was she acting so out of character?

She shifted toward him and handed him the phone without making eye contact. Seconds later she turned and hopped down from the Jeep. He watched her as he put the phone to his ear. "This is Buchanan."

"I need to ask you to keep an eye on Villa." Brock's voice sounded strained.

Erica strolled to the other side of the road, her eyes focused on the river, her forehead creased in a frown. She clenched and unclenched her fists as if trying to calm her nerves.

"Why? What's wrong with her?"

"Nothing's wrong with her. She gets a little sensitive around murder scenes."

"Sensitive?" His temper snapped. "I just saw her freak out. She looked like someone was stabbing her to death." He roared. "You call that sensitive? Wanna tell me what's really going on, Sir?"

Brock sighed, a low, tired sound. "Villa is fine. If at any point she can't do the job I will personally see to her. Until then, do as you're told. Keep me informed of any developments."

The phone went dead. *Fuck*! Trent slid out of the Jeep intending to question Erica, but the sound of Ramirez's footsteps on the gravel path became louder.

Ramirez held a black book in his grasp. He dropped it in the back seat. The book bounced once before settling on the cushion. "I got the victim's journal. If anything can give us a clue about her life, this would be it." With a lift of his chin, he motioned toward Erica. "I could scent her fear as you passed me by. Is she all right?"

Trent wished he knew. All he smelled coming off her was panic and fear. He didn't like either. In fact, his animal was all but going crazy to come out and see to her safety. "I don't know."

"You know I would never interfere between you two, I know what she means to you, but I'm here if you need help with whatever's going on with her."

"Thanks, man. I know I can count on you."

While they watched her, Erica turned, slowly making her way back to the Jeep.

"You all right, Villa?" Ramirez grinned. "Dead people's rooms freak you out too, huh?"

Trent glowered and watched Erica's lips quirk in a smile.

"You have no idea, Ramirez. Let's go to the hotel. I'm exhausted." She sat in the back, leaned her head into the headrest and closed her eyes, effectively shutting them out.

By the time they reached the small hotel, Trent was ready to strangle someone. They stopped at the diner on the other side of the motel before finally making their way to their rooms.

On a normal day he'd love a burger, a beer, and a little relaxation in his room. But after the afternoon's events, food was the last thing on his mind. Their rooms were adjacent to each other, which made it easier to meet up in the morning or work until late. Ramirez and Erica, room keys in hand, walked ahead of him to their doors. Trent was still fuming, not knowing what to make of what had happened to Erica.

"Well, I'm calling it an early night. I'm tired and need some sleep. I'll see you both in the morning. Good night, guys." Erica shut her door before anyone got a chance to reply.

Trent let himself into his room, paced, took a shower, and paced some more. He turned on the television, but all his mind saw was Erica, gripping the comforter in the victim's bedroom, choking on tears, and begging in fear. It made no sense. Just remembering made his jaw clench. Mindlessly, he flicked through channels, nothing catching his attention. The sound of the shower running in Erica's room held him entranced. After a while, when he didn't hear the water any longer, he figured she'd finished and decided it was time to question her.

He threw on some shorts and knocked at her door. She seemed unsurprised to see him.

"I'm really tired, Trent. What do you want?"

Something was definitely wrong when she didn't call him by his last name. She'd always made it a point to keep that barrier between them, stopping them from getting too personal. Good. Maybe now they could get to know each other better. And while it would take some work, he hoped he could soon—finally—have his mate by his side all the time. He strode in, stopped in the middle of the room, and turned to her.

She shut the door. Exhaustion was evident in her face, and the lingering scent of fear wafted up to his nose. Guilt nagged him to let her rest, but the questions running through his mind didn't leave him alone.

"What happened today? And don't give me any bullshit, Erica. I want to know why you reacted the way you did in that bedroom. I need to know what was happening to you. So come clean. What's wrong?" He hoped she'd open up and tell him the truth, whatever that was.

She leaned into the closed door and folded her arms over her chest, pushing her breasts to the neckline of her low-cut tank top. "I have no idea what you're talking about."

Anger simmered inside him and spread

through his veins, until he was ready to shake her. He knew what he'd seen. Even if he couldn't smell her lies, he'd know she was keeping things from him. He'd seen sheer horror in her eyes. He'd also seen a scared woman, a woman begging for help, a woman traumatized by something. What bothered him the most was that he knew that wasn't the first time she'd suffered that way.

"Stop lying to me. I was there, I saw you freak out holding that bedspread. You were shaking, begging, as if someone was tearing you limb from limb." He stalked toward her. She flinched. And he was tempted, more than tempted, to drop the questions, but he had to know what was going on. How could he help make the situation better for her?

As he got closer, her stance turn rigid, her jaw clenched, and her lips pursed. "I don't know what to tell you." She shrugged and looked down. "I freaked out a little, and that's it. I don't even remember most of it now."

Her arms unwound and lowered to her sides, hands curling into fists. She raised her face, one brow arched high. She was still defensive, and he needed to know why.

"Why are you lying? Just tell me what's wrong. Stop acting as if what I saw today was no big deal." He softened his tone to a plea. Shifting closer to her, he lifted his arms, placing them on either side of her head, palms flat on the door, caging her in. "I want to help you. Let me."

Erica glanced up into eyes the color of dark chocolate and wondered what the hell else she could do. Trent was like a dog with a bone about her episode in Lisa Summers's apartment. She had a feeling that no matter how much she tried to dismiss him, he wasn't going to go for it. It was difficult enough for her. She still had to get her mind back in order, but all she kept hearing was the dead girl's screams inside her head. Trying to get her nerves back under control was an exercise in restraint and aggravation. She needed some sort of distraction or she'd lose her mind. The grief inside the victim had been much stronger than anyone she'd ever come across.

Anger and frustration bubbled over inside her. The pain Lisa had suffered made her lash out at Trent. "You want to help me?" A bitter laugh, brimming with her aggravation, escaped. "You can't help me." She ducked under his arms and started to dart away from him, toward the bed. "No one can help me. Nothing can help me. Just go."

Loud steps sounded behind her. She should have known that he wouldn't leave. He grabbed her left upper arm. After a quick tug she found herself facing him, their bodies flush against each other. She tilted her head back to look into his eyes, and her breath caught at the tenderness she saw there. He cupped her face in his hands, the warmth of his palms suddenly spiking a flame in her veins. The indecision and concern in his eyes made her heartbeat double in her chest.

"I can't."

Her mind lost track of the conversation. She focused only on his lips, the sexy scar she wanted to kiss, and how much deeper his voice sounded. "Can't what?"

"I can't just go." He trailed a thumb over her cheek. The action not only held her in a trance but woke every pleasure cell inside her.

His intent was clear. In a movement so fast she didn't get a chance to blink, his lips were on hers. An instant fire burst in her veins and rushed through her body, pooling at her groin. Her hands crawled up his naked torso, tracing muscles, memorizing every delicious inch of hot flesh. She whimpered in the back of her throat and opened her lips to his invasion. Possession, domination, and desperation were all the things his expert tongue brought to the surface.

The hands cupping her face moved down, trailing her bare arms, around her back, until he was groping her ass over her pajama shorts. He gripped her cheeks and ground his cock into her belly. The steel length of his shaft sent moisture straight to her pussy. Her hands raked his shoulders, up his neck, and fisted the short strands of his hair.

Neither of them wanted to stop their fervent kiss for air. She would gladly die of oxygen deprivation if it meant staying exactly as they were. The heat from their bodies mingled to create a cocoon of blazing need. Every swipe of his tongue in her mouth increased the burning inside her, making her blood boil and her pussy drench with arousal.

A distant ringing broke through their cloud of desire. It was then she realized she didn't want him to go anywhere. She craved for him to stay, to kiss her, to give her enough passion to override the pain she still had lingering in her mind. They broke apart as if torn from each other by invisible hands. She wanted to keep holding on to him, but she pried her fingers open and stepped away. His gaze burned her flesh, trailing down her body.

Both panted like a pair of teens after their first make-out session. She watched him clench his jaw and lick his lips, rubbing that sexy tongue over his scar. Tight, feral hunger turned his face into a mask of need. His nostrils flared, and storminess filled his eyes, turning them glowing brown. The way he devoured her with his gaze made her panties even wetter and her nipples tighten into pebbled buds under her tank top.

That look! *Dios.* So possessive, hungry, and wicked, it made her consider running back into his arms and asking him, no begging him, to help her forget.

It pained her, but she turned away from him and headed toward the bed. The cell phone rang again, louder, almost trying to tell her that whatever was going on wouldn't go away. She sat down and stared at the screen. Brock. Trent stood there, watching her. She pressed the button to return Brock's call, put the phone on speaker, and noticed Trent take steps to close their distance.

"Erica?" Brock sounded concerned.

She knew he was wondering how she was handling what she'd seen. They couldn't discuss that now. Trent was in the room with her and she didn't want him to know.

"And Buchanan." Trent added, before she had a chance to say the words herself.

"Good. I won't have to make two calls." Brock sighed.

Trent sat down on the foot of the bed. The movement made her lean into his side. Her entire body screamed with longing wanting his hands on her and her hands on him. Oh how she wished they could go back to where they had been moments before.

She cleared her throat, attempting to calm the ragged racing of her heartbeat in her chest. "What's going on?"

"We found a new victim."

Fear slashed through her body. Sweat gathered in her palms, and the room spun momentarily. God, she was going to be sick.

"Who is it?" Trent asked, still watching her.

"The girl that went missing before Lisa Summers has been found. Gina Torres. Freshman. Same school. Looks physically different than Summers."

"What are the circumstances of her death?" She finally found her voice, although it was hard to get the words out from under the iceberg chilling and numbing her throat.

"I've sent the pictures we have to your secure emails along with the file." The sound of paper shuffling filled the line.

She opened her mouth to speak, but Trent got his words in ahead of her. "How was she found?"

Brock's somber tone was the only noise inside the small motel room. "We got a tip. Like I told you both before you left, I had a feeling Summers was not victim number one. If I'm correct, it was probably Gina. Someone called it in to 911. She was left in a public place. The placement of the body mimicked that of Summers. Open arms and legs, displaying the scars and bruises, completely naked."

"You mean she was being shown off just like Lisa?" Erica replayed the crime scene shots in her head. Her mind whirled with questions and visions of Lisa Summers. "Do we know yet if they had anyone in common?"

"Too soon to tell. We just got the call about an hour ago. You both know what to do. You can go see the body in the morning. For now just get some rest."

Erica removed the phone from speaker and placed it by her ear, knowing Brock have some other personal questions. Questions she didn't want Trent listening in on.

"Are you okay?"

Brock had always been that way with her. Since she had met him on her first day in the academy, he'd taken her under his wing. She'd been scared, but he'd introduced himself and had never been far way, helping her cope with the new environment. He taught her she could count on him, even if it had taken her years to realize how honest he was, how much of a friend he was. She'd always wanted to be part of the bureau, but being in Brock's team was better than any job she could have imagined.

"*Calmate*. I'm fine, Brock. I'm a big girl you

know." She grinned, knowing he always got a kick out of her saying that. "I can take care of myself. Now stop worrying so much, it's not good for your health."

She didn't look at Trent but knew he was listening to her side of the conversation.

Brock sighed. "Don't overdo things, please. I'll speak to you tomorrow."

She shut the phone, sprung to her feet, and made a beeline for the door. Once there, she removed all traces of emotion from her face, which was incredibly hard, and turned to Trent. "I'm tired. We're up early tomorrow to see Torres's body, I need to sleep. Thank you for coming to see me, but as you can see—" She swung the door open, holding the handle in a death grip. "I'm fine. Good night."

Trent took his sweet time standing up and strolling toward her. Each move made his muscles ripple, his body calling, inviting her to feel his strength again. He stopped right at the entrance, their bodies just inches from each other, and said nothing until she glanced up at him. Her body tensed, waiting—no, hoping—that he'd make a move. He dipped his head until they were breathing each other's air, until her body temperature skyrocketed.

"This isn't the end of us."

His vision strayed to her lips. She held her breath, already picturing him kissing her and saying to hell with her words.

"This is only the beginning."

He walked out at the same leisurely pace.

It took her a moment to realize she was standing there like an idiot.

"There is no us!" She threw the door. *Estupido!* Men always had to make things difficult by causing havoc with a woman's emotions and body.

All her hormones were still racing through her, flushing her with desire from the kisses and touches he'd given her. Every pleasure cell had liquefied and traveled down to her shorts. She jumped on the bed, punched a fist into a pillow, and growled. How the hell was she supposed to get any sleep like this? And she hadn't even packed her vibrator. Dammit.

After another cold shower and some manual stimulation, she turned up the pathetic air conditioning until there was a decent breeze. Then she finally fell into a fitful and uncomfortable sleep.

THREE

The next morning dawned bright, hot, and humid. She sat in the backseat and prayed for a break in the case as they headed to the morgue. Sipping on her iced coffee, she glanced out the window. Her mind replayed everything she knew about the victim while she scanned the passing trees, small businesses, and dense forest. It was easy to ignore both men in the front, talking sports and general things she had no interest in. She yawned.

"What's wrong, Villa? Man, you look like shit!" Ramirez said from the driver's seat. The laughter in his voice only added to her misery. Great, now they were going to turn her into the butt of their jokes.

Not bothering to reply, she lifted her hand and extended her middle finger. She was too tired to tell him to fuck off. A loud smack drew her attention.

"What the hell was that for?" Ramirez complained, rubbing a hand over the back of his head, a deep frown creasing his forehead.

"She does not look like shit." Trent growled, turned toward her, and winked. "She looks like Sleeping Beauty."

"Yeah, um, I don't remember Sleeping Beauty looking like she got run over by the prince in the story."

Slap. Her lips quirked, and a smile broke free. She knew what Trent was doing, and she appreciated him for it. Fatigue beat at her muscles. However, she was so horny that if Trent let her hump his leg, she'd find the energy from somewhere.

"What the hell? You know I'm the one driving. Cut it out. I'm sorry, Villa. You know I still think you're hot."

Slap. Erica swallowed the laughter threatening to choke her.

"Now what?" Ramirez protested. "I said she looks hot!"

"I know. That's why I hit you." Trent sounded annoyed.

"Oh man, you're in deep shit, bro. Seriously, I know you like her and all, but are you blind? Poor Villa might be hot but she looks like she hasn't slept in a week." He grinned at her through the mirror.

"Boys, if you make me pull out the ruler someone is getting spanked."

"Me!" both men yelled at the same time.

She rolled her eyes and smiled. Her lids dropped closed, and she let the two men's complaints over who should get spanked lull her to sleep.

The sound of harsh breathing filled her ears. Darkness was thick around her, driving her fear, curling around her gut and settling in with a heavy knot. Someone screamed. The sound so painful, so filled with agony and anguish, that tears filled her eyes. She raised her fists and beat at the wooden wall in front of her.

"Let me out!" Lisa Summers screamed. "Please!"

"Erica!" Trent's voice seeped into her subconscious, pulling her from the dreaded darkness of her dream. Something shook her, hard. She blinked her eyes open and saw Trent's worried brown eyes. "You're fine, sweetheart."

He pulled her out of the Jeep and into his arms.

What the hell just happened? "I know I'm fine. What's wrong with you?"

He glanced down at her with a frown. "You were screaming to be let out."

They were parked in front of the Main Street store next to the police station.

Ramirez strolled out of the store with two bottled waters, stopped, and handed one to her. "Jesus, Villa. If this is how you get when you don't get enough sleep, I don't want to see you when you break night. Your eyes are all raccoon-like. You're zombie movie material for sure."

She glared at him "*Que chistoso*. Real cute."

She drank the water, but after a few sips she stopped, remembering they were about to go look at another body.

Trent watched Erica walk into the morgue like she was on death row. Her face was pale, and her lips were pursed. She curled her nails into her palms. He frowned. Had she done that before? He couldn't recall if her nerves had been that obvious the previous day. Fear came off her in waves. Ramirez, ahead of them, opened and held the door. His need to protect her, from whatever it was making her scared, made his animal pull at the skin cage. It was hard for him to breathe and took him a moment to calm his wolf and focus on the body. Her gaze fastened on the metal table holding the body of Gina Torres.

"I need a moment alone with the body." Her words were soft with a mild wobble to them.

Maybe he was examining everything she did with too much interest. She stared at the sheet-covered lump, waiting for them to do as she requested.

"I'm going to get some details from the front desk on her address. If we're here it must mean she lived nearby. From what Deputy Owens stated only people who live in this area would have been brought here. There's a bigger precinct with a large morgue one town over. Maybe she and Lisa Summers knew each other." Ramirez said and walked out.

"I'm coming too." Trent added. He headed for the door and shut it behind Ramirez. It didn't matter that he never walked out because Erica was still focused solely on the table. He folded his arms in front of his chest and stood quietly, watching her. The scent of the bleached corpse was nothing compared to the panic drifting from Erica. His wolf wanted out. He wanted to push her behind him and protect her, but from what?

She dragged her palms over the sides of her Bermuda shorts. His breath froze. Something big was coming, but he didn't know what. She raised a shaky hand toward the sheet, stopped mid-way, and cursed.

"Get a hold of yourself, Erica. *Hazlo*. You can

do this." She said, softly.

Instinct told him to go to her. He tugged the leash on his animal and kept control. The wolf wanted near her. He waited, wondering what she planned to do next. He observed while she took deep breaths, her fear diminishing slowly. Finally, she straightened her spine and pulled the sheet back. Her arm shook before the sheet was fully off the body. He took a step, stopped, and waited to see what her next move would be. Her hand shook so badly he had a hard time not rushing to her, holding her, and easing her stress. She quickly reached out and grabbed the dead girl's arms. She froze in place.

A soft, pain-filled scream filled the room. It took him a second to realize it came from Erica. Propelled into action, he was next to her in the blink of an eye. In the time it took him to reach her, she had started to shake like a leaf and tears began to rush down her face. Unsure of what to do, he did the only thing he could think of and pulled her away from the body.

Once she let go of the Gina's arm, her body slumped toward the ground. Had he not been holding her already, she would have knocked her head on the floor. He picked her up and headed toward a wooden chair tucked in a corner. Shoving papers off the chair, he sat down and held her tightly in his arms. Her features took on a sickly color, and her already-pale complexion had a waxy grey tone. She really did look like shit. What he didn't know was why.

He rocked her in his arms and called her name softly, but she didn't respond. After a few minutes she blinked her eyes open.

"What are you doing, Trent?"

"Darlin', if you want to get into my arms, you don't need to keep fainting to do it. You can ask me to hold you whenever the mood strikes without going to these lengths."

He joked to lighten the mood, but it was starting to stress him out that she kept passing out at the sight of a dead body.

She sat up and got off his lap, without saying a word or looking back at the body, and marched to the front of the building. They passed Ramirez, who she ignored. Trent shook his head at Ramirez's questioning frown. Outside she opened the Jeep, grabbed her phone, and dialed.

"Yes, it's Villa. Gina Torres was murdered in the woods. Not far from here, but I can't say where for sure. It was nighttime, so it was hard to make things out, but I got the distinct impression he wore a hoodie so she couldn't see his face. He's big, strong, and tall. He beat, overpowered, and strangled her. And he enjoyed every minute of it. I caught the outline of his smile under the hood. She's got more wounds then Lisa. His cockiness grew since we haven't found him." Her voice shook with each word. Almost as if she'd been there.

How did she know all that? Usually Brock disseminated only the helpful information to the case, never giving them the full report on what Erica's profiling was all about. He listened intently as she continued to describe the scene for Brock. Brock only asked case-related questions, but for the most part let Erica speak.

"He really enjoyed cutting her. I wouldn't be surprised if he added some post-mortem wounds to this one. It was so weird to hear him break out in laughter spontaneously. He seems to get a kick out of hearing them scream when he hurts them... I don't know how, but I get the feeling he knew both women. We have to find the link."

Trent listened while she spoke. She was back to the other side of her personality, her no-nonsense persona that everyone in the team had gotten to know and rely on. Gone was her cheeky wit, replaced by the profiler who got the job done and gave their team the edge when they needed extra help to solve a case. But he knew that the other, more vulnerable, Erica was one step away from full-blown panic. His mate needed him, and he didn't know how to help.

She handed him the phone and strolled off to the edge of the road, staring at the trees across the street.

He jerked the phone to his ear. "Brock? What the fuck is going on?"

"Buchanan watch your mouth." Brock ordered in a steely voice.

"No, you listen to me." He growled. Screw asking nicely. He wanted answers and he wanted them now. "I've watched her beg for help and sob as if something is hurting her two days in a row without an explanation. I won't even go into the passing out or how pale she looks. What I want to know is what is going on, and how do I keep it from getting worse?" A sick, jagged sting knifed at his stomach. Was Erica suffering from some kind of illness? "Is she…is she sick?" The knot in his throat turned his question into a low rasp.

He could hear Brock exhale slowly on the other end of the line, as if trying to find the right words.

"No, she's not sick or dying. All I can tell you is she'll be fine. She just needs some sleep. Trust me. Take her back to the hotel, and make sure she rests." Brock sighed, his voice softening he added, "Please…make sure she gets some rest. She needs it."

Trent shut the phone and glanced at Erica. She had gone back to clenching and unclenching her fists. He finally realized she did that as a way to calm her nerves.

When Ramirez came out of the station he walked up to Trent. "So what's really going on here?"

"I don't know, but Brock says she's fine and she just needs some rest. I think she might be sick, but he wouldn't say. We're going back to the hotel."

Ramirez nodded. "All right, I'll drop you off and check out Lisa Summers's apartment again, make sure we didn't miss anything there. Then I'll stop by to see where Gina Torres lived. She didn't live near Lisa, but that doesn't mean they didn't know each other. Who knows, I may find something that breaks this whole thing wide open."

Trent prayed that would be soon, because if Erica got any worse, he didn't think she'd be able to handle it. He was going to make it his mission to get her to relax without sex. His cock was in disagreement, as was his wolf, but he was going to be a good mate and help her sleep even if it killed him. When they reached the hotel he followed Erica into her room. She lifted her brows high in question.

He shrugged. "Brock told me to make sure you get some sleep."

"I'm too tense to go to sleep."

"Don't worry. I'm here to help with that."

The flare of interest in her eyes made his decision to keep things platonic for the night an exercise in self-endurance.

"What did you have in mind?" She licked her lips.

Shit. Fuck. Shit.

She needed to sleep, and his body was strung up tighter than a rubber band. "I'm going to give you a massage, and then you're going to sleep."

Yeah, that sounded even worse when he said it out loud. He was going to touch her body, her soft, curvy body, and then let her sleep? How the hell he would accomplish that feat he had no clue. But he would do it…for her. And he'd keep his wolf from pushing him to claim her already. He didn't know why it was so important, but getting Erica back to her usual sarcastic self was his ultimate goal. It didn't matter that she would tear him a new one with her cheeky wit; he loved that about her.

"Normally I would argue with you, but a massage sounds so good right now I can't even say no." She picked up a tank top and pair of cotton short from her open case. "I'll be right back. I'm just going to take a shower."

She sauntered off to the restroom, her sexy hips swinging with each step, and shut the door.

Trent glanced down at his aching cock. It was

begging for relief. Yeah, good luck with that. He grabbed his dick through the soft cotton material of his pants and shifted it into a less painful position. After a few moments of standing there like an idiot and listening to the shower going, he sat down on the bed. And immediately jumped back to his feet.

It probably wasn't a good idea to wait for her on the bed. No, thinking of Erica and a bed in the same sentence made it hard to remember his objective. What the fuck was his objective? Oh yeah, just a massage. Instead, the cushioned chair next to the bed called his attention. He decided that was a better place to sit…and visualize her washing every smooth curve, water sliding down her breasts, her thighs, and between her legs. Holy fuck. He was going to end up with a severe case of blue balls.

Minutes later the bathroom door opened, and Erica stepped out, her hair in a bun on the top of her head. She wore a tiny tank top and short set. His cock jerked in his pants, reminding him how much he wanted to get a taste of her. The shower had brought back some of her normal flush, leaving her with lovely glowing skin. His mate was gorgeous. She smiled and brought out a bottle of oil.

"I use this oil to help me sleep," she said, handing him the bottle.

He looked down at the container in his hands, lavender. Not that he'd ever admit it to her, but he loved lavender. The scent turned him on. It was one of the few that didn't bother his sensitive sense of smell. "This is good."

She lay down on the bed. Once she was on her stomach, she looped the strings on the tank top down her arms, baring her back and shoulders. He stared at the shoulder he wanted to bite so badly and finally claim her as his. Biting her, marking her, and making her his mate was such a big temptation he had to grind his teeth and haul his wolf back. The animal pushed on his skin, desperate to get out and take Erica for his mate once and for all. He gulped. He glanced over her body, up her legs and took a detour to stare at her ass. A few heartbeats later he met her gaze. She had a flirty grin on her lips.

"I'm ready."

Shit.

She lowered her head to the mattress and sighed.

Taking a deep breath he walked up to the bed and stared at her flawless skin. He opened the bottle and dropped some oil into his palm. The soothing scent of lavender immediately filled the room. He rubbed his palms together until the oil heated and then splayed his hands over her shoulders. Working the oil into her flesh with smooth strokes and circular motions, he squeezed, molded, and pressed into her muscles. He started to feel somewhat confident in his ability to handle the entire massage without dying of a never-ending hard-on, until she started moaning. At first it was a small hitch in her breath, but then it turned into full-blown moans. And she wasn't quiet.

"*Mmm.* That feels *so* good," she whimpered.

Imagining her saying the same thing while he slid in and out of her body had him gripping her skin a little rougher than he intended. She groaned, and his erection throbbed. Every time she sighed or moaned his cock swelled some more in his pants. Every breathy groan out of her lips pushed him to continue imparting all the pleasure he could. Her moans torturing his mind and body weren't much fun, but who cared? Screw sanity, he wanted her to continue sighing in bliss.

"Trent." She whispered his name so low he almost didn't hear her over the pounding of his heart in his ears.

He stopped. Before he had a chance to do anything, she flipped on to her back. Her tank top hung precariously over her breasts, looking like it would reveal them at any moment. Goddamn.

"Sweetheart..."

He tried to keep his voice calm, but damn. She looked like a fantasy come to life. Her eyes were dark pools of passion. Her pink tongue flicked out and lavished her plump lower lip with a slow lick. The scent of her arousal was intense, and he knew she was wet and ready just for him. She gave him a smoldering look, filled with need and so much desire, sweat trickled down his spine.

"I want you." She lifted her arms, and her hands went straight for his hair, gripping the short strands and pulling him down.

The floor could open up and the bowels of hell appear on earth, and he wouldn't care or be able to stop from tasting her lips again. Hunger for her made him turn rough. Her open lips gave him an easy entry into her sweet depths. His tongue plundered, tasted, dominated, and possessed her. Too much had been worked up between them, and he was beyond thinking. It was time to feel. She pulled him down closer, until his body draped over hers. His cock ended up nestled between the warmth of her open legs.

Passion exploded inside him. The kiss turned wilder, desperate and consuming. He should stop. He should stop right now. Her whimpers grew, and he envisioned ripping off the tank top. He trailed his hands up her sides and grabbed her hands, stopping her fingers from twining with his hair. In one of the toughest battles against his instinct to be with Erica, he pulled away from her.

It was hell, but he didn't want to be a booty call. He'd wanted Erica for a long time and would not settle for some quick tumble as a means to relieve stress. No matter what she believed, he had feelings, and most of them were telling him this was not the right time. Erica was more than a quick lay. She was his mate.

"Erica, you're tired."

She moaned and kissed his jaw, ignoring his words. Her tongue flicked over his neck, and he almost forgot why they shouldn't continue.

"Please… I need you." She whimpered into his neck.

His cock wanted to kill him for what he was about to do. He lifted off her body and watched her open her unfocused eyes. "You need sleep. I'll see you in the morning."

He lowered his face to level with hers, placed a soft kiss on her furrowed brow, and walked out.

He knew she was confused. He'd rather face her anger at this dissatisfaction now than face her anger for having taken advantage of her later. That wasn't the way he wanted to start his relationship with his mate.

"So, you look like you got shit rest, Sleeping

Beauty." Ramirez said from the driver's side when Erica slid into the backseat of the SUV. "What the heck do you do at night? If you tell me you've been sneaking out of your room to go clubbing I'm going to be so jealous."

She growled and placed her sunglasses over her tired eyes, effectively shutting both men out. She was a fool. Trent had been coming on to her for years, and when she finally decided to give in to his playboy ways he walked out! What the hell was wrong with him? He was the biggest player she'd ever met, and he had turned her down.

"Leave her alone, Ramirez. Let's see Gina Torres's apartment," Trent snarled. The vindictive part of her was quite smug over how tired he looked. Good. It made her feel a little better to know she wasn't the only one who hadn't slept well.

"Brock and Donovan will be heading this way tomorrow." "It seems the two victims may have had someone in common. An ex-boyfriend."

Erica stared blindly out her window and thought of both victims. Thankfully, their screams hadn't kept her awake. Her own sexual frustration had her staring at the ceiling fan all night. She'd been torn between knocking on Trent's door and demanding he fulfill her sexual needs or just hitting him for leaving her in that sad state. She sighed.

Trent had the charm of any man raised as the youngest with four older sisters. He always talked about how they doted on him. He developed a charm that never failed to get him into whatever panties he wanted. Women were drawn to him. He made each one feel like the most important woman alive. He could make the sourest woman smile. That was the reason Erica had worked so hard to keep an emotional distance from him. Although that part hadn't been too difficult, the sexual interest drove her crazy most of the time.

"Did Brock mention if the ex is a suspect yet?" Trent asked.

"No," Ramirez replied. "He said that he wants us to view Gina's apartment, see what we find. Maybe something definite connecting the ex with both victims, but other than that he said there's no news. He also said Donovan is looking into the victims' cell, email, and social networking records. Apparently they were both heavy into Facebook, Twitter, and Badoo."

"What about online dating?" Trent's question caught her off guard.

Erica jerked her head toward the front and looked at Ramirez. For some reason she hadn't thought of the murderer as someone from the online dating world, but that didn't mean he couldn't be. The truth was she wasn't all seeing, and the more possibilities they took off the table, the easier it became for her to narrow it down.

She watched Ramirez shake his head in a negative. "I don't know. I guess we can have Donovan check it out, but do you really think these college girls, in a town full of kids their own age, would go on online dates? It seems pretty useless to me."

Erica nodded in agreement. "You're right, Ramirez. But a lot of college students use Facebook as more of a dating site than a networking site. So you need to keep that in mind. We need to find specific people they've both interacted with that may be connected."

"Yeah that's what I thought as well."

"Ramirez, did you happen to look through Lisa's date book? Or journal?"

"I did," he groaned. "I've never read so much gushing about a guy in my life. Oh and the petty disputes over her old friends being jealous were exhausting."

Erica perked up in her seat. "What guy was she gushing about? And what were the friends jealous over?"

"The guy was the ex-boyfriend, Derek Holmes, and she didn't say what they were jealous over, just that they were."

She mulled over his words as they reached the

place Gina Torres had called home.

Ramirez parked outside the large apartment house. Erica dropped her cell phone in her pocket and moved to open the door, but Trent was holding it open before she had a chance. She looked up into his eyes and saw determination there.

He held out his hand to help her out of the Jeep. "Erica—"

She shook her head. "This is not the time, Trent. We have a case to solve."

There was enough hurt inside her that she would rather break her neck throwing herself out of a burning building than take his hand. She jumped down from her seat, glanced up at his handsome face, turned her back, and marched away.

Erica made her way up the sidewalk, taking in the area. All of the structures appeared to have been farmhouses that were converted to multi-apartment houses. She knocked on the door to one of the large houses. An older woman with silver-white hair in a bun greeted them. She made five-foot-three Erica feel like a giant. The old woman had to be a little less than five feet tall and weigh around a hundred pounds, if that. Erica knew she wasn't skinny, but Ms. Lipkin was tiny, and she felt like a chubby amazon next to her.

"You must be the FBI folk I was told were coming along to see Gina's room." The old woman said. "My name is Hazel Lipkin. Gina was one of my boarders and the sweetest girl in this house."

Erica was caught off guard by the loud voice coming out of the small body. Ms. Lipkin glanced directly at Erica, offered her hand, and smiled. When Erica shook her hand, she gasped at Ms. Lipkin's tight grip. The tiny woman was strong.

"Hi, I'm Erica Villa. Yes, we're from the FBI. These are my colleagues, Trent Buchanan and Tony Ramirez." She pointed to the men at either side of her.

The old lady smiled, first at Trent and then at Ramirez. "You get to work with these handsome young men over here? I'd never be able to get any work done with this kind of eye candy."

Erica grinned, glancing from one man to the other. They were both preening.

"They're not all that."

"This one over here reminds me of my first husband, Mauricio. He was what they call a Latin lover. What a man." Ms. Lipkin sighed while glancing at Ramirez. She gave him a wink and then turned to Trent. "But you, my boy, you remind me of my third and final husband, Jack. He was a handsome devil, loved getting on my last nerve, but was the most loving man I ever met, God rest his soul."

Erica watched Trent's smile widen. He then turned to look at Erica as if to say, "See? Even this lady can tell I'm awesome." She rolled her eyes and shifted her attention back to Ms. Lipkin.

"Alright. If you just follow me I'll show you Gina's room." Ms. Lipkin strolled back inside, everyone following behind her. Erica took in the open entryway and looming stairs to the second and third levels.

Ms. Lipkin jerked to a stop in the middle of the foyer like a tour guide would their group. "This was formerly a farmhouse, as I'm sure you already figured out. My parents decided to turn unnecessary bedrooms into small studio apartments and rent them out to college kids. It worked so well they kept it that way for decades. When they passed I took over and continued to work the same system."

Erica noticed there were multiple photographs hanging on the walls. Each one was of a group of kids around a Christmas tree with Ms. Lipkin by their side.

"Those are taken every year for the holidays." Ms. Lipkin must have noticed Erica's interest in the photos.

"Do you offer cooking along with the room?"

Trent asked Ms. Lipkin, glancing around the room. "I know you mentioned studio apartments, but I'm sure some of these kids, if not all, aren't interested in cooking or cleaning."

Ms. Lipkin, who had been walking beside Trent, patted his bicep. "Smart, strong, and handsome. You're a keeper." She grinned. "For an additional fee we offer breakfast and dinner along with laundry services." She glanced at Ramirez, shook her head, and sighed. "You'd be surprised how many of these kids offer double so their clothes are clean and there's food for them."

Erica fell behind when they started heading up the stairs. She turned. Trent was waiting for her. He grinned. "You heard the lady. I'm a keeper."

"Hah. She's only saying that because she doesn't know you." Erica huffed. She started to move up the stairs when he grabbed her by the arm. Being one step higher than him on the stairs put them at almost eye level.

"Erica—"

She put her hand over his mouth.

"I don't need any excuses. I offered, but you didn't want me. There's no need to beat a dead horse with a stick. Can we just forget it ever happened?"

He covered the hand over his mouth with his own, pressed a kiss into her palm, and then placed her hand over his chest.

"I never said I didn't want you. I said you were tired and needed to rest." He cupped the side of her face with his other hand and looked deep into her eyes. "But be very clear, I want you. And I will have you. What we have hasn't even begun, and it's already consuming me."

He dipped his head and kissed the tip of her nose before she had a chance to stop him. She was frozen in place. He stepped back, smiled, and pulled her up the stairs to join the others.

She was too stunned by his words and actions to do much more than follow in shock. Trent, the womanizing playboy was acting...romantic? It didn't seem possible, yet he was. Is he actually worried about her? When she glanced down he was still holding her hand. He grinned and winked at her dumbfounded expression.

When they reached the third floor, Ms. Lipkin stopped. She pulled out keys from her pocket and unlocked the door. "This is Gina's room. As instructed by the police, we've kept it shut, and no one has been allowed inside." Her gaze focused on Erica. "Not that any of my other girls really want to go in there. The boys are more curious." She glanced down at the watch on her right wrist. "Speaking of which, did you want to speak to any of them? They should be coming down for breakfast soon."

"Yes. I'll leave you two to look at her room, and I'll go down with Ms. Lipkin to question the others in the house. I might learn something. Who knows? Maybe one of the residents knew Lisa Summers." Ramirez looked from Trent to Erica. He winked at Erica and followed after Ms. Lipkin back down the stairs.

Erica knew she was staring at the door handle as if it were a snake ready to bite her. But she couldn't help it. She was still exhausted and didn't think her body was energized enough to see any glimpses and dissect them with a focused mind.

"Don't touch anything." Trent ordered. "I will not have another episode of you passing out on me. Got it?"

Her stomach churned and she nodded. There was no way she wanted to see until she was no longer dead tired. Besides, her emotions were too worked up over Trent's words.

FOUR

Trent held the door open. Erica walked into a very messy room. She scanned the piles of clothes on the bed, shoes all over the floor, and books laying everywhere.

"Wow. And they say men are pigs," he joked.

"I thought the saying was men are dogs?" She took careful steps in her trainers. Keeping her hands at her sides, she avoided touching anything. Her first impression was that Gina was a busy girl. She walked over to the dresser. A photo of the victim was on the mirror. She was dressed for a masquerade, though she held her mask off to her side. Two tall guys stood to either side of her. Another two men were right behind her. Only one of the men wore a mask.

The masked man had his face turned away. Erica couldn't make out his features, but the silly face Gina made filled her with sadness. What a terrible end for such a lively girl. Sticky notes littered the frame of the mirror. All seemed to be appointments, dates, and things to do. The notes were written in a kind of shorthand that only the writer would understand. Gina had used initials for names.

"Hey, I think I found something." Trent called out from the other side of the room.

Erica turned to her left. He stood there with a journal or appointment book. She quickly made her way to his side and was a few steps away when she tripped over a pair of heels. Trent reached out to steady her at the same time she moved to grab his hand. Instead of his hand, she grabbed hold of the journal. In a flash, she watched the last moments of Gina's life play out like a horror movie scene. Because the victim's energy was at the highest at the moment of death, it was one of the first things that came to her. She saw it all just as Gina had.

At first Erica was confused over what she was seeing. Loud music played, and she couldn't hear herself think. It was some kind of dark room. A musty smell filled her nose, almost like a wet cellar or a basement. The unfinished room had bad lighting, visible pipes, and drywall mid-construction. The coldness of the room made her shiver. That's when she looked down at her body.

She was strapped to a bed that was positioned in an angle. Tight belts bit into her skin, holding her down. She didn't know why she was naked, but panic started building inside her. A sound made her turn and squint into the darkness. A tall, dark, covered figured watched her. He was big, wearing dark jeans and a hoodie. Gina's vision was blurred. Erica knew Gina had been drugged, but it wasn't until then she realized how heavily.

When he shifted, she blinked and squinted harder, but the view of him grew fuzzier. He held something in his hand. A scalpel. Gina's heart started beating so fast she thought she was going to throw up. Fear took over and made it even harder to think clearly. The hooded figure laughed when she started screaming to be let loose. She struggled against the binds holding her in place, but it was no use. He'd strapped her so tight she couldn't even feel her arms or legs.

The figure moved closer, lowering his head by her ear and whispered, "You're going to regret your choice."

He sounded excited. As if he were enjoying admitting that to her.

A sharp blade cut into her stomach. Raw pain filled her mind. She screamed at the top of her lungs, begging for him to stop.

Erica jerked her eyes open. The first thing she saw was Trent's concerned face.

"Erica?" He called her name, his voice rough with emotion. "Sweetheart, please tell me you're OK."

They were in the living room of Ms. Lipkin's boarding house, along with Ms. Lipkin and Ramirez, who were watching her with worried frowns.

"I'm fine. Really," she added when he gave her a dubious look. "I need a pen and paper."

She sat up and pulled her cell phone out of her pocket. She knew she sounded deranged, but she had to make notes and talk to Brock before the details she'd gathered turned into one blurry nightmare.

"Please?"

"I'll get it." Ms. Lipkin patted Ramirez's arm and left the room.

She dialed Brock while Ramirez stared at her in confusion. Trent scrutinized her, more concerned than angry, which she was grateful for. The last thing she needed was him pissed at her for passing out on him again.

"Erica?" She placed a hand over the mouth piece on her cell phone and addressed the others in the room. "If you don't mind, I need a few moments please?"

Ramirez and Trent moved through the open door into an adjoining salon. She could still see them and they her, but she was able to speak softly and keep things between her and Brock.

"Hi, we're at Gina's apartment house. Here's what I gathered. She knew the person who killed her. Which is a big break. He drugged her, so it was hard to see clearly where he took her, but I got the sense the location was isolated. There was a strong musty scent, so I think he had her in a basement or cellar, or some other place that can smell of water. He is big." She ran a hand through her drooping ponytail. "The man we're looking for is tall, muscular but not a body-builder type, and he's into hurting women. He carved those words and laughed, actually laughed while doing it."

She pulled the elastic band off her hair and tied it back up into sturdy ponytail, all while holding the phone between her ear and shoulder. "He tortured them for a while before finally bringing it all to an end. I couldn't see his face clearly. This wasn't random; this was a grudge. Hell, this was more like his personal vendetta. I think maybe they rejected him somehow, and this was his way of getting back at them.

Ms. Lipkin returned with a pad and pen and gave Erica a glass of water. "Are you OK?"

"Thank you, yes. Just low blood sugar. I forgot

to eat." She lied. Guilt nagged her since the poor old woman had been so kind. Ms. Lipkin returned to the other room and chatted with Ramirez. After sipping some water, Erica started taking notes of what she remembered. Still holding the phone to her ear, she wrote and spoke to Brock. She knew everyone was staring at her from the other room like she was some kind of freak, but she was used to it.

Her entire life she'd been different. Even her mother had gotten rid of her because she couldn't handle Erica's "gift." Erica had smashed her give-a-shit-o-meter a long time ago and knew how to block people out so they wouldn't hurt her. She lifted her gaze to connect with Trent. He nodded sharply and continued to watch her quietly. She focused on the conversation again.

"We are on our way and should be there by late this afternoon or early evening. Make sure you don't touch anything else before you get some rest. You need to stop overdoing it. If you don't I may send you on medical leave." Brock's voice was strained, his worry tightening his vocal cords.

"We don't have time for me to wait."

"What did the ME report say?"

"He didn't sexually assault any of the victims, but still... Brock, this person is out there. He knows we're looking for him." She stood and walked to the window overlooking the entrance. She lowered voice some more. "I can feel his interest in the investigation. I have a bad feeling he's going to up the ante and do something bigger soon."

It was more than a feeling. Normally she wouldn't touch during a murder investigation unless absolutely necessary, but this time she was touching a lot more than she had anticipated. Her heartbeat sped when she remembered the laugh, the satisfaction he gave off when he had hurt Gina. She'd gotten a glimpse into the evil that consumed the predator. Because he was a predator. He got off on making women hurt, and he wouldn't stop until she caught him.

Trent glanced around the dining room table and was glad Ms. Lipkin had offered them lunch. Erica appeared ready to fall over from exhaustion. He still didn't know exactly how her profiling worked, but he had a feeling that by touching things she got an idea of what happened to the victim. It made her an indispensable part of the team and was probably why Brock made her his second in command on this case. What she did was already way more involved than what he had expected. He had no idea she had some kind of psychic power. Clearly she was some kind of empath.

"Thank you so much for lunch, Ms. Lipkin." Erica smiled at the older woman.

"Oh, please, you're more than welcome. It was no problem to add a few more plates. We always have an excessive amount of food in this place. Kids are always coming in and out, and we need to make sure everyone is fed."

Color slowly returned to Erica's face. Trent started feeling better once he saw her hands stop shaking. It was obvious she needed rest, and he'd be damned if he would let her work herself into an early grave. His wolf growled. He'd find the killer and then take his mate on a much-needed break.

"Did Gina speak to you about any of her boyfriends?" Erica leaned close and gave Ms. Lipkin a conspirational wink.

Trent hadn't thought to ask the old woman that, but it was a good question.

Ms. Lipkin pursed her lips and passed the coleslaw to Ramirez. His face creased with disgust, and he handed it on to Trent. Trent, who had never been a fan, gave it to Erica. She didn't even look down and passed it straight back to Ms. Lipkin.

"Not really. She only ever mentioned one guy. Derek Holmes I think was his name." She passed the rolls around the table, and after everyone had grabbed one she smiled and continued. "She went out with him…" She shrugged. "…but then so did most girls in this house. Poor Gina didn't realize he was a ladies' man. After a few dates she saw through his playboy act, but before she had a chance to confront him, he broke up with her. He'd found a new one who was ready to ignore his womanizing ways. Trust me when I tell you, I've had a few girls whose hearts he broke while they were living here."

Ms. Lipkin sighed and shook her head.

"Ms. Lipkin, did Derek ever try to communicate with Gina after they broke up? Maybe pursue her again with the intent to get back with her?" Ramirez placed two pieces of fried chicken on his plate.

Trent stared at the dish with fried chicken and almost drooled. It smelled so good he wanted to keep the chicken, but when he looked up Erica was glaring at him, hand outstretched, waiting for the platter. He grinned, grabbed two pieces, and passed the large plate to Erica.

"No. The boy is much too in love with the idea of girls chasing him. He's a junior at the college. His younger brother is a lot more serious from what I understand, but I've never heard of him getting chased by all the girls. Derek is always with a different girl and loves it." Ms. Lipkin appeared genuinely disgusted with Derek's actions, but didn't seem to be holding anything back.

Trent made a mental note to see the ex-boyfriend and find out more about him. The picture was starting to look pretty clear to Trent. There were two dead women. Only one man had dated both girls. And they had no other suspects. It was too much of a coincidence in his book. He was about to take a bite of his chicken when he happened to look at Erica. He stopped mid-bite. She had just put a piece of chicken into her mouth, closed her eyes, and moaned.

"Oh, god. This is the best fried chicken I've ever had." She groaned and slowly opened her eyes. He gulped and stared. She glanced straight at him and licked her finger, twirling her tongue around the digit slowly.

He was ready to take the rest of the chicken back to the hotel, strip her, feed her, and then bring her to orgasm with a different piece of meat. He tried to remember she'd fainted earlier, but his cock didn't give a shit. He wanted her, and if he didn't have her soon his balls would probably fall off. She was doing it on purpose, but he couldn't seem to get his brain to tell her to cut the torture and eat like a decent girl. Of course, the sexual tension they'd both been under was making him feel like every move she made was intended to torture him.

"Don't you just love some good meat?" Ms. Lipkin grinned at Erica and then at him.

What the fuck? Was the old lady helping Erica in her cruel game with his mind and, well, his cock? Because he fully believed Erica was trying to work him into a state of blue balls, though at this point it was more like purple balls. He'd gone way past blue after the massage from the night before.

"You have no idea how hard it is to find good meat, Ms. Lipkin." Erica blew him a kiss.

Holy crap he was going to hell. Straight there with a first-class ticket, because he wanted to fuck Erica on the dining room table right in front of Ramirez and the old lady. Screw sensibility, he needed to get Erica out of her clothes. On a bed. Or in a car. Or a wall…or pretty much anywhere they could be alone. And fuck her until his cock no longer hurt from pent-up arousal.

Trent glanced at Ramirez, but the idiot was so involved with his food he'd completely missed the entire thing.

"So, er…Ms. Lipkin, do you have any idea who would want Gina dead?" He tried to bring the conversation back to the victim and help his brain and cock get back under his control.

Ms. Lipkin snickered, knowing what he was doing, and decided to take pity on him. Thank god. "No, she was really pretty but also really popular. She wasn't stuck up like a lot of the girls that come from the city. Her family is from the Bronx, and she was the first to go to college, so they were all chipping in to help her with her expenses. She babysat on weeknights for the college professors in the area."

Erica's gaze lifted from her plate. "Do you know which professors she babysat for?"

Ramirez seemed to come back to the present and added his own two cents. "I'll find out and also see if maybe any of them are connected with Lisa Summers."

Trent nodded and finally started eating. Now that everyone's attention was back on the case, it was easier for him to get his appetite back. His appetite for food, that is. His appetite for one sexy, curvy brunette never seemed to go away. In fact, it felt like it was growing stronger and much more desperate by the minute.

After lunch they went back to the motel to discuss their impressions of Gina Torres. They met in Erica's room, since it was the only one with a table to spread their victim information out on. Notes and files littered the entire table and bed surface. The motel room was much smaller than they had anticipated.

"Okay, so here's what we know," Erica started, taking charge, "Gina and Lisa both went out with

Derek Holmes. Gina was killed first, but Lisa was found first. Both show the same type of wounds, at the same exact locations on their bodies. Except Gina had some extra wounds that Lisa didn't. Which leads me to believe he was still hesitant went he killed Lisa. But with Gina...he went further. He added wounds and carvings that Lisa didn't have. But they are still the same type of wounds, and I can tell by the style that both women were definitely killed by the same person. Not to mention *I* know they were both killed by the same person," she said absently and stared at the picture of Lisa's body.

His gaze connected with Ramirez's, who frowned at her last sentence. Trent's next item on the agenda was finding out more about how she got her information. The dark circles under her eyes indicated she was exhausted, but her voice and speech were clear and concise. He had the urge to grab her and hold her. She looked so vulnerable, staring at the dead girl's photo.

"We also know that Gina babysat for professors at the college on certain nights." Ramirez bounced on the bed. What, was he four?

"Right," Erica said, snapping out of her trance. "So what we need to find out is if any of those professors were linked with both victims. I know we have an ex-boyfriend we need to go question, but I want to know if there is anyone else the girls might have in common."

Trent could see the wheels turning behind her tired eyes. If the killer wasn't the ex-boyfriend, who else could have access to both women and have a motive to kill them?

"Alright." Ramirez put the papers back in the files on Erica's bed. Once he'd cleaned the bed of the multitude of pictures and notes, he placed the remaining documents on the chair by the stacked table. He walked to the door. "I'm going to go make some calls. Find out more and give Donovan a shout-out to see if she's got anything on the social media side."

Trent watched him leave. Once the door shut behind Ramirez, he turned back to Erica. She stared at Gina Torres' photo. Because she'd been staring at it, Ramirez had left it behind on Erica's bed when he'd cleaned up. Thankfully she hadn't decided to touch the thing.

Trent took a deep breath and decided to ask the question that had been burning his tongue for the past two days. "So how exactly does it work?"

She lifted her gaze from the photo and blinked at him with a puzzled look. "How does what work?"

"Whatever it is you do to find out about the victims." He saw her start to shake her head in a negative and continued, "I know it has to do with touching their things, but I can't figure out what it is you see." He grabbed the photo and placed it back in the corresponding file. Somehow he knew if he left it out she'd continue to stare at it.

She gulped and clenched her hands into fists. Finally after a few moments, she looked back up at him. The anguish he saw in her eyes made him go to her, grab her hands, and hold them in his own.

"Tell me." He drew circles on her palms with his thumbs, hoping to help calm the distress he saw on her face. The scent of her anxiety diminished with each stroke of his thumb.

She took a deep breath. "It's very simple, really. I touch something of the victim's, and I see their last moments alive. It could be anything from how they got killed to who killed them. Whatever they saw, I see. If it's a missing person who's not dead, it's usually their last lucid memory from a few hours past. I don't see things in real time, which is why it's so important that when I see someone still alive, we try to find them that way."

He thought about what she said for a moment. "Do you feel their pain too?"

She jerked, turning back to him, and nodded. "Yes."

Fuck. No wonder she'd been crying every time she touched the victims' stuff. She was reliving their deaths in full color, complete with a side of physical and emotional torture.

"How long have you had this…ability?" He wanted to know more about the woman who fascinated him like no other ever had. He needed to get to know her before he bound her to him.

"Always." She pulled her hands from his grasp and started to pace. He was sure she didn't even realize she was doing it.

"Is that why people think you profile?" That was what Brock told everyone in the department. That Erica was the profiler in the team, and she led every investigation with whatever she pieced together. No wonder they depended on her so much. She knew what happened, but it came at a pretty hefty price.

She continued to pace to the door and back toward the bed, stopping only to look at him and then slowly turning away. "Yes. Only Brock knows what I can see. He's…he's aware I'm more than just a profiler."

Jealousy made his blood burn. She was his. His woman. His mate.

"What's the side effect of this…this ability of yours?" He knew sleepless nights were a given. She'd never looked as exhausted as she had in the past forty-eight hours.

Face scrunched in thought, she hovered by the bed. "What do you mean side effects?"

"What does it do to you to see what you see?"

"Well…"

It seemed she didn't want to share, but he wasn't stopping now. "I know you can't sleep. So what else is there?"

Erica turned away from him and spoke while walking back to the door. "It's not that I can't sleep. It's that I keep seeing the victims in their last moments over and over again in my dreams. It doesn't make for restful sleep to keep seeing that."

What the fuck? She wasn't lying. Her words shocked him immobile. "You mean you don't just see them that one time? You keep seeing the same thing over and over again?"

"Kind of. The initial contact, the first time I see while touching something is a crisp, clear view, almost movie-like, and it gives great detail, if that's what the victim saw. But after that…" She bit her lip in thought before continuing. "…I guess we can call it first touch, the images become distorted, blurry, and blend together to form flashes of cries and pain. Almost like a compressed set of layers of the entire event. It can be tiresome to keep trying to make the view as clear as it had been in first touch, but all you have is indistinct and confusing images. It muddles in my mind and gives me migraines."

He stared at her. Deep sorrow pierced his heart with every word out of her mouth. "How long do you see these visions for?"

"It usually takes days, sometimes weeks, for it to stop." She creased her nose, still not looking at him. "So when I see more than one in a short period of time it…it's exhausting. I feel their pain over and over, and it drains me. Trying to shut out the screams and the visions takes a lot out of me."

Holy fuck. The woman was insane to keep her mouth shut all that time. He wondered if she was getting any time with the paranormal psychiatrist. Brock had made him go to therapy the time he'd tried to sink his claws into a predator who'd abducted a woman and kept her hidden from her family.

"You mean to tell me you've been dealing with this on your own and you didn't think to share it with me? I could've helped."

He was hurt that she suffered in silence. All the years they'd worked together and he had had no clue she had been going through that. It made him want to kick his own ass. If he hadn't been so involved in trying to get into her pants, he would've noticed something sooner. Instead she'd always worked alongside Brock, and he, Ramirez, and Donovan had been the action team. It had never occurred to him that Erica was much more vulnerable than what she portrayed.

The image she showed the world of a tough, bitchy profiler was just that: an image. Underneath it all she was suffering, and it hurt him to know that. He'd decided the moment he met her that he'd allow her to come to him when she was ready. It was clear she was his in his mind, but he would never push her. He was done waiting.

She seemed confused by his anger. "How would you have helped?"

His heart broke for her when he realized she was genuinely confounded. She'd been dealing with this on her own for so long she didn't think someone giving her a shoulder to lean on or emotional support would help her deal. She was his mate for crying out loud. It didn't matter that she didn't know it, he did. And he needed to let her see that he was there for her, always. He walked toward her in slow measured steps, and then he stopped when he was a foot away. Her eyes widened when he lifted a hand and curled it around her jaw. He caressed her cheek with his thumb. "I would have been there for you. I could have helped you deal with it. You didn't have to do it alone."

"But...I've always dealt with it alone," she whispered, and his heart cracked some more.

"You don't have to anymore." He lowered his

face and stopped inches from hers. "Never again." He leaned in and brushed his lips over hers, their gazes locked in a tempestuous embrace. "I'm here for you, Erica. You can lean on me."

He pulled her body flush to his in a slow move. And then he kissed her again. This time with enough passion to show her how much he wanted her. He hoped she could see that she meant more to him than any other woman ever had.

FIVE

Erica sighed into the kiss and allowed her lips to soften under Trent's slow invasion. Sparks bubbled in her blood and fired her veins with each swipe of his tongue. He drew slow circles over her lips before moving into her mouth. Tingles coursed through her body, going straight to her pussy. Their tongues caressed each other in a sensual ritual that left her breathless and panting.

His hands moved under her top, tracing the curve of her waist and crawling up her sides. Urgency for him, the only man she'd been wanting for years, made her pull at his T-shirt. Her hands gripped the cotton material and lifted. He must've gotten the hint, because his hands left her body and he stripped off the shirt. And good lord was she happy to see him without the offensive cloth. She knew he was hot, like really fucking hot, but seeing all those muscles up close and personal made her want to purr.

She licked her lips while trailing each bulging bicep with her fingers. Her gaze darted up to meet his heated one.

"Your turn," he said in that deep, sexy voice that made her want to beg him to talk dirty to her. The wicked grin on his mouth was pure sin. She grabbed the sides of her tank top and pulled it over her head. His look? Priceless. His eyes zeroed in on her breasts. She was no little woman, and when she arched her back his nostrils flared. Her body was full of curves, and she had no problem with it.

Their lips met again in another scorching kiss. A kiss that deepened the strange connection they seemed to have. All this time she'd felt the pull to him. She knew there was something strong between them. Her mind and heart told her she was delusional if she thought she could deny the deep connection to Trent, but her rebellious side refused to acknowledge it. Sex. *Si*. This was only sex, because she didn't do relationships. Pushing the strange thoughts out of her mind, she wallowed in the feelings he aroused in her body.

He gripped her waist, and their bodies were

once again flush. This time the long, hard, length of his erection pressed into her belly. It made her pussy quiver in need. His corded muscles rubbed her already-hypersensitive skin, and she dug her nails into his biceps. He trailed kisses to her jaw, and she trembled. Oh, but it got better. He moved to her collarbone and stopped at the valley of her breasts.

She lolled her head back and shut her eyes. Spiky hair met her fingertips when she moved one hand up to grip the short locks. He removed her bra. In an instant his lips were on her nipple, sucking her tight little bud over and over again. Her lungs constricted with each lick and suck. She moaned and bit her lip. It was hell to keep from begging. Sharp desperation made her shove her chest into his face. He'd bitten one of her nipples, and the sensation had been divine. She wanted him to do it again.

"Oh Dios..." Her breath hitched when she looked down. The hottest man she'd seen in her entire life licked, sucked, and caressed her body. He made her feel like she was the sexiest woman in the world. He looked up, and she almost came on the spot. He nibbled on her breast, and she groaned when he stopped and unlatched from her swollen nipple.

"I want you." His voice was so rough she could barely make out the words. He gripped the waistband of her pants, but he didn't unzip and open them. Instead, he watched her with expectation.

"I want you too." She panted. "Now."

Just in case he'd decided to stop, she moved her hands to the waist of her pants, unsnapped, and unzipped them. Then she watched him pull them and her panties down her legs. The sudden indrawn breath he took made her smile.

"You're so fucking hot."

He glanced up, licking his lips. Her pussy throbbed at that moment. Any thought not related to Trent licking her heat shut down in her mind.

"I swear I could look at you forever," he whispered. His gaze roved over her naked body.

He stood, kissed her again, and lifted her into his arms. She wound her arms around his neck and wrapped her legs around his waist. His hands went straight to her ass cheeks and ground her to his cock. She whimpered and released his lips. Passion licked at her skin. She moved her mouth to his jaw. Biting down on the scruffy flesh turned her on like nothing ever had. She wondered if she had a vampire complex, because licking, sucking, and biting him made her aroused beyond the point of rational thought. She dug her nails into his naked arms. He moved with her in his grip, and soon she found herself on her back on the mattress. It was hard to breathe. She watched him strip off his pants with unwavering interest.

His body—and what a body it was—was defined with muscles and bronzed skin, made her lick and bite her lip in expectation. She mentally caressed down his big frame his long, thick cock. A shiver ran up her spine, and she gripped the sheets under her hands.

"Like what you see?" He smiled wickedly.

"*Si*, I do. But do you know what to do with that?"

It was time for him to put up or shut up. And she really wanted him to put up.

"Baby…I don't have protection."

"It's ok, I'm on the pill, and I'm clean."

"Are you sure that's what you want?" He frowned. "We can wait. I wasn't expecting this to happen now between us. I had hoped, but I hadn't expected. I've never been with any woman without protection." He cleared his throat and a soft blush colored his cheekbones. "I want you to know that I'm also clean. I don't get human diseases, but I still get tested. One can never be too careful."

She grinned. He was truly concerned for her choice to go without a condom. "I've never been with anyone without one either. I'm ok with this.

Now, show me what you've got."

He grabbed her ankles and pulled her body down to the edge of the bed. She could only stare while he got down on his knees and placed her legs over his shoulders. Air froze in her lungs. He wrapped his arms around her thighs and lowered his face to her pussy. At the first swipe of his tongue on her clit, she bucked.

"Oh my god," she moaned and refused to follow her body's command to shut her eyes.

He lifted his head from her throbbing core and smiled. "No, sweetheart. It's Trent, but you can call me god if you want."

Before she got a chance to give him a sarcastic reply, his tongue dipped into her entrance, and she was lost to the bliss he was imparting on her pussy. He licked around her waxed lips and proceeded to fuck her with his tongue. She panted and ground her hips down, closer to his face.

"Please…"

She whimpered when he did a slow trail around her clit with his tongue. He flicked it twice, and then she felt his fingers rub up and down her pussy, wetting them with her dripping heat. Feeling his calloused fingers over her sensitive flesh turned into a new point of pleasure. After a moment he dipped wet fingers into her. She groaned and tightened her hold on the sheets. Her hips rocked on his face involuntarily.

He sucked on her clit while his fingers curled and thrust in and out of her. It took very little for her to go over the edge. Her heart pounded in her ears, each beat a fierce, wild gallop. Tension unraveled inside her, pushing her headfirst into an all-consuming orgasm. She screamed when a wave of pleasure rushed through her.

Panting like she couldn't get enough air in her lungs, she blinked the haze of happiness away and looked down to see one sexy Trent jerking his cock; beads of liquid seeped from his slit and slid down the sides. She scooted up on the bed and kept her legs wide open for him. Some kind of non-verbal communication happened. Her insides melted at the blazing look he gave her.

"Fuck me." That had not been what she'd planned on saying, but it worked just as well.

"Baby, what I'm going to do to you is way more than fucking." He grinned and crawled on the bed, stopping once he'd kneeled between her thighs. He trailed a finger around her pussy, dipped it into her wetness, pulled it out, raised it to his lips, and licked. Blood fizzed and popped in her veins. The man certainly knew how to add kindling to her fire.

While she watched, he gripped his cock,

rubbed the tip on her pussy lips, and coated his shaft with her moisture. He slid into her in a deliberate, drawn-out move. She groaned at the slow torture. She contracted around his thick length with every inch he went deeper inside her. He was big, and he stretched her in a way that made her feel every nerve ending in her pussy sigh in bliss. Once he was fully embedded in her, he lowered, his arms bracketing each side of her and caging her in. Without waiting for his command, she lifted her legs and wrapped them around his waist, locking them in place behind his muscular ass.

Emotions she wasn't familiar with filled her when he gave her a soft look. He lowered his head, and their lips meshed in a wet tangle of tongues. While he kissed her senseless, he pulled out of her and slammed back in with so much force she was glad she was holding on to his arms. Again he withdrew and thrust into her hard. And she loved it. A fine sheen of perspiration coated their skins and allowed him a smooth glide over her body. In and out he went. She pulled her lips away from his and moaned. Her nails dug into his shoulders while she hung on to him for dear life. The sound of skin slapping, grunting, and moaning filled the room with an erotic melody that increased her pleasure. The musky scent of sex overpowered and incited her body's arousal.

"Yes, more," she pleaded. The coiling tension inside her was near its breaking point, and she needed him to fuck her harder.

He quickened his thrusts until she could no longer speak and all her focus was to topple into orgasm. Trent stopped, and she growled.

"What the hell are you doing?" She was going to kill him.

The bastard just grinned and got on his knees. Still deep inside her, he lifted her off the bed and draped her legs to either side of him. He sat back on his heels and chuckled.

"Relax, you'll be calling me god again in about a minute. I'll take it in English or Spanish, your choice."

Erica curled her hands around his neck and dug her nails into the back of his head. His hands held her by the waist, and he lifted and then ground her over his cock. She whimpered at the new sensation of him filling her even deeper. Holding on tight, she rocked her hips on him and moaned with every wave of her body.

"Oh, my —" Her breath hitched.

"That's it, love. Ride me." He encouraged and pushed her to move faster over him.

Her movements quickened to an almost-uncoordinated pace. She felt his lips over her neck, licking, sucking, and driving her arousal through the roof. He slipped a hand between her legs and pressed on her clit, flicking it with his thumb. She arched her back, her entire body shook, and an electric shiver ran up her spine. The tension inside her snapped.

"Oh, God!" The ragged scream tore from her throat.

Trent continued to rock her over him, adding to the sensational feelings going through her. He sucked on her shoulder, licking circles around her neck bend. While her body trembled from inside after that amazing orgasm, he licked her, nibbling on her sweaty flesh. He continued to rock her; his fingers dug into her hips, gripping her skin. Seconds later he ground her down, hard. Her pussy fluttered around his cock, and he bit down on her shoulder, groaning. He hugged her tightly to him and shook.

They fell on their sides, both gulping for much-needed oxygen. He pulled her to him until she was lying half draped over him. His hand caressed the curve of her ass, and he kissed the top of her head. Erica didn't know what to make of the flood of emotions going through her. She was so confused. Trent was a womanizer; she knew that. And yet here she was feeling things that weren't going to lead anywhere. They had to work together, and she didn't see how he could be trusted for anything more than casual dating.

She'd seen too much in her life to depend on a particular person. The school of hard knocks — aka first-hand experience — rivaled any Ivy League degree. There was no way in hell she'd give in to any kind of emotional pull. The last train wreck she called a relationship had ended when the accountant she'd been dating told her she needed to see a shrink. She screamed while she slept and refused to open up to him. Yeah, open up and get ridiculed like she had all her life? "You see dead people, Erica. You're such a freak." She'd broken it off with him, just like she did with every other ex who had attempted to get inside her head or her heart.

Lifting her face, she peered up at Trent with curiosity. He was giving her that soft look again, and it freaked her out. She tried to think of something to say to break the tension mounting in her shoulders.

"I never thought I'd see the day," he said, his chest still rising and falling with each quick intake of air.

"Huh?" What in the world was he talking about?

"I can't believe I was able to make you lose your tongue. This has got to be some kind of miracle. Maybe I should call in a priest in here to witness."

She sat up and poked him in the chest. "I did

not lose my tongue. And I don't want anyone witnessing what we just did, but I'll have you know I was just thinking of a way to rate your performance."

"That good?" He winked and tugged her body up, sliding over his, until their faces were inches from each other.

"It was…" She gave a haughty sniff, hoping he'd take her next word as a challenge. A definite challenge to fuck her again with the same bone-melting perfection he'd used before. "Adequate."

He observed her for what felt like an eternity. Arousal gathered inside her into a winding knot. She glanced down at the sexy scar on his lip and licked her lips.

"What did you say?" His low, rough tone sent moisture straight to her still-throbbing pussy.

"I—" She gulped. He caressed her back, moving his hands to run circles over the sides of her hips. The erection that had been lying dormant suddenly thickened to create a steel pole poking her under her mound. "I said it was adequate."

One minute she was looking into Trent's intense eyes, and the next she was on her stomach, ass up and face down in the covers. What the hell? She went to lift her head but stopped when he barked, "Don't move."

He trailed his hands slowly down her spine, over the curve of her ass, squeezing and groping her cheeks.

"So sexy." He groaned seconds before she felt his lips kissing the round globes. "So tasty." His deep voice rumbled over her hole.

Her breath abated, and she fisted the sheets in a tight grip, waiting. For what? She didn't know. She only knew that whatever he did, she would enjoy.

He licked the line that ran down her crack until he reached her slit and then back up.

"So hot. So mine." A graze of his teeth had her squirming in his hold. "Don't move. I want to eat you every way possible."

Her pussy throbbed, and moisture dripped from her sex. The feel of the bedding on her nipples made her groan and rub her sensitive tips on the sheets. Trent continued to lick, kiss, and bite her ass. When he licked his way from her puckering hole down to her wet slit again, she groaned loudly.

"Please..."

Arousal melted away any questions. She turned her head slightly and peered over her shoulder. Trent lifted back to a kneeling position, grabbed her hip with one hand, and guided his cock to her opening. He didn't hesitate and drove right into her pussy in one quick slide. Her breath hissed out while her pelvic muscles squeezed around him. They watched each other, breaths huffing, bodies burning with need. Desire curled around them in a thick blanket. The scent was so potent she wanted to bottle it and keep it forever. Her body roared in satisfaction when he withdrew and thrust back in, all the while watching her.

"Since that last one was only adequate maybe I can do something to make it better."

He slammed into her harder. She whimpered, loving every stroke of his cock inside her. The death grip she had on the sheets was the only thing holding her anchored. She dropped her face into the bedding and held on while he pounded her with each thrust. The fire in her womb roared to an inferno with each of his drives into her pussy.

"Harder," she ordered, only for him to slam right into her so far, fast, and rough her ass lifted off the bed. If he hadn't had such a tight grip on her hips she would've bashed her forehead on the headboard

"Oh, god. More."

She whimpered and propelled her ass back with each thrust of his cock back into her, making him reach deeper than she thought possible.

"Like that?" he asked and turned up the speed of his movements, jackhammering her with his cock. The mattress's squeaking sounded louder and louder, until she was sure everyone in the entire motel could hear them. Not that she cared. Right now the place could fall down around her and she wouldn't stop.

"*Si*. Fuck me faster."

His chuckle came at the same time he increased his tempo. The speed of his thrusts made it difficult for her to do anything other than try to catch her breath. Her pussy screamed for the orgasm that was just out of reach. Trent reached between her legs and rubbed her pleasure nub while continuing his wild slides in and out. The heat of his body caressed her spine. He kissed the back of her right shoulder, licking her skin with sensuous flicks.

"You're mine, Erica." He growled by her ear; his deep voice sent pricks of lust straight to her core.

"Yes, yes, yes."

"Mine!" He growled and fucked her harder.

"Oh… Yes!" She choked on a scream when she came. A rushing tidal wave of ecstasy coursed through her body. Her pussy clenched around Trent's cock in an iron grip.

Seconds later she heard him groan. He bit

down on her shoulder, hard. His fingers dug into her hips while he ground his cock into her pussy and tensed. He jerked into her repeatedly. She'd swear his cock thickened inside her, and warm semen filled her womb. The biting combined with his jerks into her swollen sex sent mini-orgasms whooshing through her. They ended up right back where they started, on their sides panting for air.

"Well?" He was out of breath.

"Goddamn. I didn't know you'd bite."

"Sorry. I—"

"Don't apologize. I must have more issues than I realize, because I liked it."

He laughed and kissed her shoulder. The kisses started feeling like licks after a moment. "So what did you think this time?"

"Okay, I can't lie. That was better than adequate…it was good."

She laughed when he squeezed her breast and pinched her nipple. Damn. If she wasn't so exhausted she'd totally continue their game. However, sleep decided to claim her, and she found herself doing something she hadn't done in a long time: allowing a man to snuggle and hold her while she fell asleep.

SIX

Trent knew the moment Erica fell asleep. Her body leaned back into his and softened under his hands. His cock, which seemed to feel right at home in the curve of her ass, lifted up with interest. He tried to will his erection away, but the fact was her sexy curves made him so hard he wanted to fuck her until he couldn't move a muscle. And that bossy attitude when she told him to fuck her harder? That just added to her overall perfection.

He wondered what his mom and sisters would think when they met her. And they *would* meet her. She was his mate. His woman. There was just no way they could have a relationship without his family finding a way to bring her into their bosom. Long-term with Erica? Yes. Both he and his wolf had known from the moment he had met her that she was special, that she was his. He had been willing to wait, but he didn't think her level of hesitancy would run this deep. It was time to step up his game and show her they were perfect for each other. She might be wary of his past, but she'd come around.

There was a knock at the door. He didn't want to wake up Erica. She was so exhausted she didn't even stir when a second knock sounded. He stood, dressed, and covered her with a sheet. She snuggled into the thin blanket and sighed. He checked the air conditioning unit so she wouldn't sweat while she slept.

When he opened the door, Brock was at the other side of the threshold.

"We need to talk." Brock didn't frown; he glared at Trent as if he'd committed a crime. He motioned for Trent to follow him outside. Trent glanced at Erica's sleeping form and quietly shut the door behind him.

"What's going on?" Trent knew he sounded brusque, but he couldn't help the jealousy he felt over Erica trusting Brock more than him.

Brock marched to the other end of the motel, where a small diner was located. Trent trailed behind him. Once inside they slid into opposite sides of a booth; the plastic cushions squealed when they sat. The place was empty even though it was early evening, and only one plump, middle-aged waitress stood behind the counter. She smiled flirtatiously, unaware some of the red lipstick had stained her teeth.

The waitress walked over to their booth and handed them laminated menus.

"What can I get you to drink, boys?" She bent forward to place filled glasses of water on the table.

"I'll have coffee, please." Brock examined the menu.

"Make that two."

The waitress took off. Brock put the plastic menu down and gave him a look like he wanted to beat the shit out of him.

"I'm guessing you finally got into Erica's pants?"

Anger made Trent grind his teeth. "That's none of your business."

"Actually, it is."

Before Trent had a chance to reply, the waitress brought their coffee.

"Have you boys decided what you'd like to eat?" She smiled at Brock and then winked at Trent. The way she spoke made the word "eat" sound like something dirty, and not in the good sense.

Brock handed her the menu. "I'll have a cheeseburger with fries. No pickles. And a soda."

Trent nodded. "I'll take the same, but make mine a bacon cheeseburger." He needed to remember to bring something back for Erica to eat. He'd order her food after they finished. No sense in bringing back cold food.

"Look, Trent, Erica is special."

Brock used his first name—something he never did. He then dumped enough sugar in his coffee to make any kid bounce off the walls. He added cream and started to stir, frowning.

"I know that. She's mine." Trent said.

"She's yours?" He stopped and stared at him for a moment. Trent knew his words conveyed the message of how serious he was for Erica. "It's gone there, huh?"

Trent added two sugars and some cream to his coffee and locked on to Brock's face.

Brock took a sip of his coffee and sighed. "I hate driving this far without caffeine. I don't think you realize just how special Erica truly is—"

"Look…" Trent tried to hold his temper since Brock was still his boss. "I know she sees things about victims and the toll it takes on her—" He stopped when Brock shook his head.

"I knew you'd either figure that one out or she'd tell you about it. That's not what I'm referring to as special. She's very important to me."

Trent ground his teeth and bit back an oath. His wolf pushed at the skin. "How important?"

Brock shook his head. "She's like my sister, jackass."

"Oh." His jealousy disappeared. "So what do you mean?"

"Erica is a very important part of our group, yes, but she's also very independent and self-controlled."

Trent ignored his cup, his interest now fully on what Brock said. "I know that. She's made it clear in all the time we've worked together that she doesn't depend on anyone."

"Do you know why?"

The waitress came back with their food just then.

She put the plates and drinks in front of each of them and curled a hand on her hip. "If either of you need anything else, I'll be right over by the counter. Just wave and I'll come right over."

She sauntered off, wiggling her butt. Trent couldn't help it. This time he did chuckle. He glanced back at Brock to find him grinning and getting ready to eat.

"No. I don't know why, but I'm assuming it's got something to do with her past." Trent put fries, ketchup, and mayo on his burger and then added the top bun. He put the massive burger straight into his mouth and took a large bite. Damn, that was a good burger. Probably made better by the fact he'd worked himself into hunger devouring Erica's sexy body.

"OK, I'm going to give you a summary so you're not caught unawares, which I have a feeling might happen. Erica was abandoned by her mother into the court system."

Trent was about to take another bite but stopped, shocked by what Brock had said. "What do you mean she was abandoned?"

Brock sipped on his drink before answering. "Exactly what I said. Her mother was freaked out that her little girl kept telling her about crimes people had committed and told the court system she couldn't handle a crazy kid. So Erica went into the foster care system."

Trent sat immobile. He couldn't believe a mother would do that to her child. "How old was she?"

"Four," Brock answered, popping a fry into his mouth.

Good lord. Could a woman really do that? A mother? It didn't seem possible to him. His mom had been both mother and father to five unruly children, but she'd never lost her patience with them. And he knew they'd done enough stuff to make a saint drop his halo and kick their asses. His father had been Alpha of their pack, but when he was killed his mother took him and his sisters and moved away. She had been unwilling to let anyone in the pack tell her what to do. She raised them among the humans. So Trent didn't see how Erica's mother could have actually given up her daughter. Trent lost interest in his food.

"What happened then?"

Brock swallowed what he'd been chewing before answering. "She went through a slew of foster homes until she was about fifteen. That's when her last foster parents had her committed."

"Wait, what? What do you mean they had her committed?" His voice rose in anger. Erica was not crazy.

Brock nodded. "Yeah. She told the foster mother that the foster dad had raped a girl who had previously stayed with them and was later found dead. Erica had found the girl's bracelet, and when she touched it she saw what he did. It created a mess for Erica."

Trent could only imagine how alone she must've felt when she told the truth and was labeled a liar and crazy. His stomach clenched, and the urge to go over to the room where she sleeping and hold her struck him. He never wanted her to feel alone again. He looked up and saw Brock eat the last of his burger. "What happened after that?"

"Well she was in a hospital for a little while. They did all kinds of tests, and Erica realized she needed to keep her mouth shut in order to be set free. Once they found out she really wasn't crazy, they sent her to a group home. But by then she'd enrolled in an early college program. One thing she'd never done, even with all the things she was going through, was let her grades slip. She was accepted into a criminal justice program and went off with a full scholarship. That's when her life really started."

Trent could sense a hidden message in there. "But?"

"But she learned not to trust anyone. When she came to the academy she was always alone, but she has a deep connection to the crime victims in a way no one else has. And from that, she could understand things about the perpetrator that no other evidence could show us. I created a new unit, a special unit, and wanted her. She was the only person who could do what she does. She sees the crime as it happened. She sees the killer."

"How did you find out about her ability if she

doesn't trust anyone?" Trent's jealousy returned.

"I knew of her past from her files, but the way they worded things, it truly made her sound like an unstable person, a psychotic who heard voices. But the longer I worked with her, the more I realized her file was filled with lies. So one night on our first big missing person's case, I handed her a photo of the victim. She grabbed it without realizing what I had given her, and you can imagine what happened next."

Yes, he could. "Scared the shit out of you, didn't it?"

Looking down at his burger, Trent decided to give it another chance. He picked it up, took a bite, and glanced back at Brock.

Brock nodded. "Hell yes. There we were, talking calmly one minute, and the next she was screaming at the top of her lungs to be let out. Thank god we were the only ones working that late, or someone would've thought I was killing her. It took some persuasion. I had to tell her how helpful it would be for the job if she told me about her skills. I was given the go ahead by superiors to create the Federal Paranormal Unit. You, Ramirez, and Donovan joined next. But I made sure to work one-on-one with Erica, alone at the crime scene or at the victims' homes. Most cases I have acted as her guardian and helped her work up to the moment of contact. I made sure she didn't push too far too fast."

"Why do you have so much interest in her?"

Brock shook his head as if trying to let him know he was taking things the wrong way. "She's got no one else. I couldn't stand seeing her live her life believing she had no one on her side. She doesn't trust anyone, but she knows I have her back."

"So what you're trying to tell me is that she's going to make it difficult for me to have a relationship with her?"

Brock laughed. "Buchanan, she's not just going to make it difficult, she's going to make it so hard you're going to think you're back in boot camp." He chuckled again like Trent's love life was the biggest joke in the world. "I like you, and I think she likes you too, which is why I'm telling you all this."

Trent frowned, trying to remember what he knew of her past love life. "But she's had other relationships before, hasn't she?"

Brock shrugged. "Not really. I know she dated in the past, but she always cut them off when they started to look for more. She's scared to trust and depend on anyone. When she thinks that's where the relationship is headed, she dumps the poor saps."

"Wait, if that's what's waiting for me, why

would you want to help me?"

"I told you, I like you, and I am pretty sure she does too. Erica is very private, but she's got this entire ice queen persona going when it comes to men. She's like a sister to me, and I want her to be happy." Brock's smile slid off his lips, his eyes taking a bright glitter Trent knew as some kind of paranormal energy fighting to come loose. "So that means if you don't make her happy I will kick your ass."

"Threat?"

"No. That's a promise."

Trent had a lot to think about. He contemplated the food that remained. His appetite had vanished, so he pushed the plate away. Things with Erica were not going to go as smoothly as he'd predicted. He knew what they had between them was special and worth pursuing. He'd never felt the way he did with her with any other woman. His mother and sisters had always told him that when he met his mate he'd know because he wouldn't be able to stand the thought of being away from her. Just imagining Erica out of his life made his palms clammy, his stomach twist, and his anger soar. He just needed to find a way around her mistrust.

He glanced up to catch Brock watching him with a smile. "I told you, she's going to be a hard one."

"She's my mate."

"Look, I know what that means to you, which is why I'm not going to give you a dissertation over your playboy past, but Erica doesn't really know what a mate means to you. I trust that you have long-term intentions with her."

Trent was no quitter, and Erica was the woman he wanted. And not just for a little while, he knew she was the right one for him. She was a prickly, sarcastic, bossy, and sexy-as-hell little harpy. Yeah, she was the perfect woman for him. His mate. "Don't worry about me. I'm not letting her go anywhere."

Brock laughed and ate the last of his fries. "OK, but you need to tell her about your little animal problem."

Trent nodded. "I plan to. Soon."

"Good. She already mistrusts people. The last thing she needs is to feel like you've been playing games with her too." He leaned back on his seat, making the plastic on the booth seat squeak. "Now that we've got that out of the way, tell me about the case. Other than what she's told me, what is your impression?"

"Honestly? I think the ex either did it or knows who did. This is aggravating as hell. The bodies have been scrubbed clean, so no particular scent is left behind. Even their apartments are so filled with stuff we can't discern a particular scent. So that's my guess. Look. Two girls went out with the same guy. They both disappear, are murdered, and there's no other links between them. And we know that they were killed by the same guy."

Brock nodded and handed his plate to the waitress, who had popped up out of nowhere.

"Can I get you anything else, handsome?" She gave Brock what Trent assumed to be her version of a sexy smile.

Brock grinned, probably because of the lipstick, and pointed to the pie display. "Do you have apple over there?"

"Sure do. Want it warmed up with some ice cream?" She licked her lips, and Trent almost burst into laughter.

"Yes, please." Brock winked at the woman, and she sighed as she walked away, completely ignoring Trent in her haste to get the piece of pie.

Trent shook his head. "That's messed up, man."

"Hey, if it gets me some food without spit in it, I'll gladly smile and wink at anyone handling the stuff that's going to go in my mouth." Brock was unapologetic.

He did have a point.

"Did Donovan find out anything else about our victims and their social media?" Facebook, Twitter, and all the other social sites made things even harder for them. Donovan would have to search through both of their profiles and check for anything strange.

"Donovan said Lisa might have been dating a professor, but that's not definite. She's still going through emails, texts, and chat logs."

At the mention of a professor, Trent jerked his gaze to Brock. "Gina Torres babysat for one of the professors in the college."

Brock's brows lifted in obvious interest. "We'll need to find out who he was and if it was the same guy."

Anita returned with Brock's apple pie a la mode, and Trent ordered Erica's cheeseburger. He made sure to get her curly fries instead of regular and to ask for it cooked extra crispy, just the way she liked. When Brock gave him a you're-so-screwed grin, Trent glowered. Yes, he'd been so interested in his mate that over the years he'd learned everything he could about her. Don't ask him how, but he knew she loved to eat ice cream when they couldn't find a missing person. And the flavor had to be mint chocolate chip.

He knew she liked to read romances when she thought nobody was watching. That one he'd found out by sheer luck. She'd dropped her electronic reader, and he'd bent down to pick it up and seen the name of the book. He'd looked it up and found out it was the kind of sappy romances his sisters liked to read. Erica might not believe in relationships, but she liked to read about happily ever after. He also knew she was allergic to most flowers, except tulips. She loved the color blue and cried at romantic comedies. Yes, he was a peg or two short of a stalker, but this was his woman. The woman he'd been giving time to come to grips with him. He'd been so drawn to her from the beginning it was hard not to go out of his way to find out more about her.

"Donovan said there were a few names that popped up repeatedly on the Facebook pages, and she wanted to check them out before saying whether she thought anything might come of them."

"Something about this just doesn't sit right. Those two girls were nice, outgoing girls. Nobody seemed to have anything against them. So who could've done that? Even the woman where Gina Torres rented said she didn't think Derek Holmes would do something like that."

Brock stopped mid-bite, frowning in concentration. "Derek Holmes, that's the ex-boyfriend?"

Trent nodded. "And he's also under the belief he's god's gift to every new girl in that college."

Brock laughed. "Sounds like someone else I know."

"Hey, I resent that. I do not think I'm god's gift to women." Trent drank the last of his soda and placed the glass on the table with a thump. "I know I am."

Once Erica's food was ready and Brock had finished his pie, they paid the check. The waitress returned with the receipt and handed it to Brock. Her phone number was written in the back of the paper with a message that read: "call me, hotstuff."

Trent laughed the entire way back to the room.

SEVEN

Erica woke up to the smell of food. When she opened her eyes, Trent was sitting beside her on the bed with a Styrofoam container in his hands.

"Hey there, Sleeping Beauty. I thought you might be hungry, so I brought you something to eat."

God, the man still made her horny as hell. Now that she knew how good he was in the sack, she'd never be able to look at him and not think of his tongue or cock in her pussy.

When she sat up, the cool air made her nipples pebble. Trent and his sexy smile had made her forget she was naked under the sheet. She pulled the blanket up to cover her breasts. Her eyes strayed down to his crotch where proof of his straining erection was visible. Pushing the hair away from her face, she peered back at his eyes.

"Feel free to drop the sheet, beautiful. I like looking at your body." He grinned.

Did he ever stop? Oh, hell. She didn't want him to. The man was fantastic for a woman's ego. "Thanks, but I think I'll get dressed."

She gave him a pointed look.

He just sat there, his smile widening some more. "Go ahead."

Yeah, he was definitely shameless. The crazy part was that she liked it. She was still all kinds of horny for the big pain in the ass, and now he wanted to watch her dress. Talk about torture in the first degree. And why did the prospect of him looking at her send excitement shooting through her? Erica looked Trent straight in the eyes, dropped the sheet, and got up from the bed.

A sensual rush went through her when she saw him lick his lips, a hungry spark darkening his eyes. They were inches away from each other, and his face was level with her breasts. She took a moment to torment him with the vision of her full breasts then turned on her back. The groan she heard come from Trent was enough to make her grin. She bent right in front of him, ass high in the air, showing off her wet pussy in the process, and picked up her panties.

She straightened and walked toward the bathroom. Forget feeling bashful; she wanted him to want her.

"Erica?" His voice was hoarse.

"I'm going to take a shower." She stopped at the door and looked over her shoulder at him. His gaze was fixated on her ass. "Feel free to join me." She added, walked over to the tub, got in, and shut the curtain.

She heard him curse while removing his clothes at record speed. The sound of his footsteps when he neared was drowned out by the loud clatter of the water running. Cool water kissed her skin, and she stood under the spray for a few moments before Trent was pulling her wet body to him.

Their lips met in a blazing kiss. His hands roamed around her waist and squeezed her ass. She moaned into the kiss, raking her nails over the back of his shoulders. Urgency to have him made her push him back until he ended up with his back on the slick tiled wall, away from the spray.

Fire shot through her, arousal rising to scorching heights. He sucked her lips, nibbling at the corners. She pulled away from him and glanced into his sexy eyes. Taking her sweet time, she placed butterfly kisses over his jaw. The slight facial hair growth made her pussy moisten even more. She loved the rugged look, especially on Trent. It was sexy as hell. Gliding her hands down his body, she placed kisses on his torso until she reached his nipples.

When she licked around the tight bud and grazed her teeth on it, he groaned and thrust against her stomach. His rock-hard erection pressed hot on her belly. She continued her journey down his body, biting, sucking, and licking her way down his muscles. The journey ended with her on her knees before him. His nostrils flared, passion etched onto every line of his face.

His cock called her attention. She grabbed the thick length in a tight grip and sucked the mushroomed head into her mouth.

"Oh damn." He pulled her wet hair away from her face, holding the long mass in his fist while he watched.

She licked a slow trail from his balls up the vein on the underside, until she was once again popping the head into her mouth. Trent's groans had her moving a hand between her legs to play with her pussy.

"*Yesss*. God, you're fantastic."

Hollowing her cheeks tight, she sucked him in as far as possible. Trent started to thrust into her mouth, sliding and gliding over her tongue. She kept a firm grip on the base of his shaft the entire time. She bobbed her head repeatedly and twirled her tongue over him. His dark, enigmatic gaze kept her entranced, pushing her to pleasure him further. Moving one hand to fondle his balls, she jerked and sucked him faster in her mouth.

"Just like that. Suck me."

It was an incredible turn-on to hear his dirty words. She moved her fingers into her slit and finger-fucked herself while tightening her grip on his dick.

"Fuck!" He thrust his hips into her mouth and tensed. Warm semen slid down her throat, and she swallowed, their gazes still locked while she sucked down his cum. He was standing there panting while she licked his cock clean and stood.

The minute she straightened, he kissed her. Tongues rubbed, and her already throbbing body became one giant, aroused mass of nerves. He pushed Erica's back against the tiled wall.

He got down on his knees and nudged her thighs wide open so he could fit his face in between them. She looked down and watched him lick a trail from her slit to her clit. Her breath hitched, and she leaned her head back, focusing only on what his lips were doing to her body. He grabbed her breasts and squeezed her nipples while licking her pussy.

"Mmm"

She moaned, loving the tweaking he did to her nipples. Her need for release made her widen her legs for more. She placed her hands over his on her breasts and guided him to pinch a little harder. It was enough to make her groan and roll her hips on his face.

She slithered a hand down and spread her lips open more so Trent could have easier access to her clit. The moment his lips wrapped around the tiny nerve bundle, she started riding his face. He moved a hand between her legs and soon two of his fingers were fucking her while he sucked on her. He growled. The sound sent vibrations into her pussy and made her gasp. After another, harder, pinch on one of her nipples, she soared.

"Oh, God!" Her body shook. Every single part of her felt overdosed on endorphins. Air panted out of her lungs, and if Trent hadn't stood and held her in his arms, she would've slid down the wall into a boneless puddle on the tub floor.

His arms held her tight while he kissed her face. Their lips locked into a slow, sensual kiss. Trent pressed her body so close to his, their hearts were beating in duplicate gallops. On top of that, he decided to wash her with so much gentleness she wanted to cry. No one had ever been that sweet or nice to her. He cleaned her and himself and wrapped a towel around her body. Whenever she looked up at him, he would just lean down and kiss her again. The kisses, soft flutters that enticed her body all over again, freaked the hell out of her.

"Alright people, settle down," Brock ordered the group sitting around empty pizza boxes. They were in the living room of the cabin they'd relocated to that evening.

He'd decided to get them a private space where they could work in a more secure area and spread out. Everyone got their own room, although Erica noticed Brock had given her a room next to Trent, and they had to share a bathroom.

Jane, who was the only one missing from the meeting, walked into the room a moment later. A deep shade of red covered her usually peachy complexion, and her narrowed eyes focused on Ramirez. Uh-oh. She dropped a folder on the coffee table and continued toward him. Ramirez sat on an easy chair, and Donovan didn't seem to care that there were others in the room. She caged Ramirez in by placing her hands on the arm rests and leaning forward until their faces were mere inches from each other. Her dark red hair fell down her back in long ponytail, still wet from a recent shower.

"Listen up, Ramirez. I don't give a shit how many women you have back in the department. I also do not care how sexy you think you are, but if you ever walk into the bathroom while I am showering without knocking again, I will cut your balls off and feed them to stray dogs. Do I make myself clear?" She punctuated each word with enough force to make even Brock's brows lift.

Erica grinned and folded her arms over her chest, ready to enjoy the show.

Ramirez, the pervert, looked into Donovan's green eyes and then right down her tank top. "Sweetheart, there's nothing you have that I haven't seen before."

The minute he said the words, the silence became so intense you could've heard a pin drop.

Donovan's indrawn breath showed how ready she was to kill Ramirez. Erica turned to check out Trent's reaction. She could not believe Trent was smiling like a lunatic and elbowed him in the ribs.

"Ouch," he grumbled.

"It's not funny. What he did was completely inappropriate," she whispered.

"I know, but I bet it was still fun."

"Stay away from the bathroom when I'm in there, or I won't be held responsible for what happens." Donovan stood straight and glanced at Brock. "I mean it. I will hurt him if he does that again."

She was practically vibrating with anger.

Brock glared at Ramirez. "You heard her. Knock on the door before you go in there. Don't make me have to write out reports over murder. You both know that I don't tolerate anything that makes anyone uncomfortable. When it comes down to it, our team's base is mutual respect. We are still professionals."

Donovan sat in a sofa opposite Ramirez and glared at him the entire time. He, on the other hand, smiled and winked at her. When Trent gave Ramirez the thumbs up, Erica smacked him upside his head.

"Seriously, babe," he said while rubbing the back of his head, "you need to stop it with the violence. You know I'm ready to do your bidding. If you have some kind of fetish, I'm willing to explore that, but we have to agree to some limits."

Erica rolled her eyes and tried to bite back a grin, failing miserably. He was like a big kid, and it boggled her mind that she liked him so much.

"You two..." Brock pointed to Erica and Trent. "Cool it. Must I give lessons on what is and isn't appropriate work conversation?"

Erica blew Brock a kiss, but he just shook his head. "Alright, now that everyone has been reminded that we are still working a case, not participating in Spring Break, let's get back to business." Brock turned his gaze to a still-fuming Donovan. "What'd you find out for me on the social networking sites?"

Donovan took a deep breath and picked up the folder she'd dropped on the coffee table. "Lisa Summers and Gina Torres had four men in common. The subjects with the most intimate familiarity with our victims are two. One is Derek Holmes, who dated both girls within a six-month period. The other man was Professor James Green."

"Professor? Is he the one Gina babysat for?" Ramirez leaned forward in his chair.

Donovan pursed her lips. "Yes. Gina babysat for James Green at least twice a week. Apparently his wife travels a lot, and he always hired Gina to watch his kids when he gave evening lectures."

"And how did Lisa know him? Was she in his class?" Erica asked.

Donovan glanced down at her notes before she answered. "She was last semester, but this semester she was his lover."

Trent whistled low. "Wow. I'm kind of jealous

I didn't become a college professor and have hot young girls hitting on me." He pouted and placed his arm over Erica's shoulders. She elbowed him in the gut again for his words. "Ow!" He rubbed his ribs and gave her a hurt look. "Am I going to have to take you to rage-a-holics? Because I bet I know better ways to work out our differences." He winked.

"Oh, come on." Donovan sighed in complaint.

"Focus, people, focus. Let's get back to this case. What other people do they have in common?" Brock took a sip out of the soda can.

"The other two are Anthony Holmes, Derek's younger brother, and Richard Thompson." Jane said looking over her notes.

"Who's this Richard Thompson guy?" Brock asked.

"I don't know yet, but he seems to be really popular in the college. He's friends with almost 20 percent of the student body on Facebook." Donovan flicked a lock of stray hair behind her ear.

"OK, we're going to have to interview these guys. Let's start with the ex and the professor and work our way from there." Brock looked toward Erica and Trent. "I'm sorry Villa. I'm going to have to ask you to work on this without me a little longer. I have to meet with the governor. He wants a personal visit with me on the status of the case. You and Buchanan take Derek Holmes. As the ex, he's our most likely suspect." He glanced over to Ramirez. "You will visit Professor Green." Then he turned to Donovan. "Donovan, find out more about Richard Thompson and Anthony Holmes."

Erica walked back to her room. She had so much on her mind she didn't pay Trent any attention. She shut the door to her bedroom before he had a chance to follow her. It was time for her to get some space and think about the case. She wondered if one of the four men was the killer. Thoughts of the victims and what she knew of the killer rushed forth in her mind.

The man was tall, built, and strong. She wished she could've gotten a good view of his face or heard his voice, but unfortunately with both victims he'd been in shadow. She couldn't make out the voice over the noise.

She thought back to Trent. He'd been himself and at the same time more attentive toward her. The silly, sexy part of him would never change, but now he seemed even more interested in pulling her into his jokes and making her laugh. She wasn't sure what was going on inside her when it came to him, but she knew that the feelings growing for him were unlike anything she'd felt for any man before.

What the hell was wrong with her? She knew better than to put her faith in a womanizer like Trent. But none of the women who had dated him in the department ever complained about him being anything other than a gentleman. Just thinking of him with someone else made her blood boil.

What was she going to do about him? He has seemed more attentive. Could he be thinking about them in terms of more than sex? Hell, she was thinking about them as more than just sex. It was sweet—and scary as hell. She shook her head at the ridiculous thoughts. It wasn't a good idea for her to start thinking long-term.

EIGHT

Trent lay on Erica's bed, waiting for her to come out of the bathroom. He heard her puttering and grinned, imagining what she'd be wearing when she came out. Anticipation made his cock jerk in his boxers. He glanced down at them with a frown, wondering if he should take them off too. It's not like she hadn't seen him naked, and from the looks of it she'd enjoyed the way his body looked. He decided to stay as he was, in his boxers and nothing more, while he waited.

She'd gone ahead of him and shut her door, which he assumed was her way of telling him to keep out. Lucky for her, he could reach her bedroom through the shared bathroom. So he'd quietly walked through while she was showering, stopping only for a moment to listen to her hum, and then had made his way to her bed. There was no way in hell she'd be sleeping alone again. He wanted to protect her, guard her, and hold her. His new goal was to be there for her and soothe her whenever the nightmares attacked.

When the bathroom door opened, he grinned. His sexy, mouthy woman wore a tank top that showed off her puckered nipples as if she'd had nothing on. Long dark hair was piled up into a messy bun on the top of her head. Her lower body called and held on to his attention. She was wearing a pair of boy-short panties that looked like they were made to entice him into doing all kinds of things to her. The material of her underwear pulled at the crotch, making his mouth water.

Erica frowned when she saw him lying on the bed. "What are you doing here?"

He tried to think past the urge to strip her and lick her entire body until she came, screaming his name. "It's time to go to bed."

She lifted her brows. "I know that."

"My bed is wherever you are."

"That's sweet. Now get out."

"No."

"Trent."

"Erica."

"I'm tired. I need sleep."

"Come on, baby. I'll make it worth your while." He waggled his brows.

She looked like she was trying not to giggle. "Need. Sleep."

"Ok, so we'll sleep."

"You make this so difficult."

"It doesn't have to be difficult. Just come to bed and let me hold you. That's all I want to do. Don't you understand that I love being near you. That every moment I spend next to you makes me happy. Holding you in my arms is enough to give me peace."

Her gaze softened and she smiled. "Talk about hitting below the belt. Fine, you can stay. But I warn you, I sometimes have nightmares."

She looked away from him, as if embarrassed.

"Don't worry, sweetheart. I'll protect you from whatever bothers your sleep."

She climbed on the bed and sat back on her heels looking at him. "Thank you."

He felt like they were having a critical and special moment.

"For what?" He couldn't figure out what she

was talking about this time.

"For taking care of me." She looked down at her hands and frowned. "I know it's hard to understand what's happening when I touch something, but you really helped me. I don't want you to think I don't know that."

Trent smiled and felt his heartbeat quicken. She'd opened up, even if only a little, to him. He grabbed her hands and pulled her to him. She lost her balance and landed over him, her hands on his shoulders and their eyes locked on each other. His hands slowly trailed from her waist, up her back until he was cupping her face. Confusion was clear in her gaze. He wanted to reassure her that he'd always have her back, but knew she'd probably dismiss his words as fluff.

"Erica...you're special...more than anyone else has ever been."

Her eyes widened, the crazy beating of her heart accelerating above his. "I don't need promises or sweet words, Trent. I just want *you*."

She lowered her head to kiss him. He wanted to take things slowly this time. For her to feel like what they had was more than a quick fuck, more than something temporary. He kissed her slowly, licking her lips until she dug her nails into his chest.

"I need to tell you something…"

"Not now, I don't want to talk right now."

"But this is really important." He said between kisses.

"No. Now kiss me."

He dipped his tongue into her mouth, and she mewled, seeking more, but he kept the deliberate measured pace. Their tongues caressed and twirled, mating and rubbing in a sensual dance. He traced the smooth contours of her back to the edge of her tank top and under the hem to feel her silky flesh. Heady arousal shot through him, turning his already painful erection concrete stiff.

She sat up, her crotch rubbing on his shaft, and wiggled until she straddled him. He watched her nimble fingers remove her tank top. Passion heated his blood with each move she made. She stood up on the bed, her legs to either side of him, and dropped her panties. A sensual smile slid across her full lips, making his heart trip in his chest. She crouched down and straddled him again. His hands went right to her breasts and squeezed them. She lolled her head back and pushed her chest into his hands, softly whimpering for more.

Trent lifted his torso off the bed and latched his lips on her nipple, sucking the swollen bud into his mouth. Her breath hitched. Again he did it, this time with the other. Back and forth he went on licking her soft mounds repeatedly.

"That feels so good." She glanced down at him.

She rolled her hips over his cock. Dampness from her pussy soaked his boxers, making the wet material rub erotically between them. She pushed him on his back, caressing his chest with her breasts. "I can't wait any more." She licked his lower lip.

Holy fuck was she sexy.

"We don't have to." He pushed his boxers down his legs when she lifted off him.

She yanked the boxers off.

Needy desire gave her eyes a glazed appearance. "Yes. I want to feel you, all of you, inside me now."

A moment later she straddled him, gripped his cock in her hand and licked her lips. He held her by the waist, his eyes glued on the sensual scene before him. She rubbed the head of his dick on her wet folds, sighing with each stroke. Heat raged inside him, took over his veins, and overpowered logic. He needed in her. Now. She lubricated his cock with the honey dripping from her slit. Their gazes locked, and she slid down and impaled herself with his shaft.

"*Yesss.*"

Both moaned in unison, their bodies locked tight, his cock pulsing inside her fluttering sheath.

Her palms on his chest, nails digging into his flesh, she used him to balance.

"Trent…"

She rolled her hips in a circular motion. Perspiration gave her body a golden sheen, an almost ethereal, sex-goddess type of glow. He groaned with each wiggle of her hips, gripping her tight.

"That's it. You're so sexy. Ride me."

Her breasts bounced, calling his attention to the tight peaks begging to be kissed. She did a body wave that ended with her grinding her pussy on his pelvis.

"God, sweetheart," he groaned. "That's so fucking hot."

He cursed when she did it again, clenching his teeth in an attempt to keep from coming before her. She threw her head back, and he swore she had no bones. Each body wave jerked his dick in a slow glide inside her slick walls. It was fantastic. She increased her speed, moaning and whimpering louder at the same time.

She sat up a little straighter and squeezed her breast with one hand, rolling her nipple between forefinger and thumb. Down her slick body, she moved her other hand between her legs to flick her clit with her middle finger.

"Oh my god, I'm—" Her breath hitched, her

body tensed, and she whimpered his name.

Trent's mind went completely blank. His sole focus: to enjoy the ride.

"Hell yes!" He grunted and lifted his ass off the bed, needing to sink his cock deeper into her wet grip. Air propelled out of his lungs at warp speed, while he released inside her tight channel.

Erica fell forward onto his chest. They both struggled to breathe, but he felt so satisfied he couldn't stop the stupid grin that worked its way onto his face. He caressed her spine and drew circles on her ass cheeks. She had the perfect body, made for long hours of loving. He was glad she wasn't into the being-super-skinny hype.

Too many times he'd gone out on a date with a curvy woman and seen her skip a normal meal because she was dieting and felt the need to lose the curves god had given her. It made no sense to him. He liked his women with enough meat on them that he could have something to hold on to. He squeezed Erica's ass. She had the sexiest body. As soon as his brain stopped drooling over it, he'd get her to ride him again.

Erica slid off him, but when she gave him her back and tried to move away, he just pulled her flush against his front and spooned her. She wiggled her butt and fell asleep with his arms around her waist.

Trent woke up in the middle of the night to the sound of soft whimpers. After a moment of intense listening, he realized the cries were coming from Erica. She'd turned toward him at some point in the night. Since she'd warned him about the possibility of a nightmare, it didn't catch him unawares. She hugged him. His arm pillowed her head. The low lighting from the bathroom allowed him to see her face clearly. Tears fell from the corners of her closed lids. It was hard to watch. Wrapping his other arms around her, he held her close.

"Shhh, sweetheart," he whispered. "It's alright. I'm here. Relax, love."

He rubbed her back in what he hoped were soothing motions and kissed her forehead. Her whimpering quieted, but he continued to hold her, unwilling to let go. He stayed that way, with her in his arms, and whispered that all was fine until she relaxed in his hold. Pain had filled his heart when he'd seen her cry in her sleep. It felt good, right, to have her in his arms.

"So you're sure the ex is at the police station?" Trent glanced at Erica's face. She frowned, deep in concentration.

"Yes. Apparently when the father heard that

his son was in our list of suspects he wanted the kid cleared and sent junior to answer any questions we have. The kid isn't very happy we've kept him waiting. He promised to call the news stations and every politician his daddy is friends with." She sighed, turning to look out the window.

Upon nearing the police station, Trent thought about what they needed to ask. Erica had mentioned that she'd know, once she spoke to Derek Holmes for a few minutes, if he was the killer. What he didn't tell her was that he'd also know if Derek was the killer. All he'd need to do was ask, and if the kid was lying he'd smell it immediately. He had to sit and talk to Erica soon about his shifter abilities.

When they got to the station, he cut off the engine and turned to her. Just before she had a chance to pull the door handle and jump out, he grabbed her, stopping her movement.

She glanced his way, her brows lifted in question.

"I don't know what you plan to do in there, but I don't want you doing anything that's going to make you pass out. Brock and I want you to stay away from anything that will create stress." He and Brock both felt the need to ensure she didn't overuse her ability.

She stared at him for a moment. "I'm fine. I

rested."

Trent realized she hadn't agreed to his request. "Promise there won't be any John Edwards stuff with you and the kid."

She chuckled, a low, throaty sound he loved, and shook her head. "There won't be anything strange with the suspect. I just need to talk to him."

That was going to have to be enough, because she didn't seem like she'd offer any other promises. Trent jumped out of the Jeep and followed behind her into the small station. Inside, the same deputy they'd spoken to before waited by the counter. Deputy Owens smiled the moment he saw Erica.

"Ms. Villa, nice to see you again."

"Deputy Owens." She shook his offered hand. "We're here to speak to Derek Holmes."

One thing he loved about his woman was that she didn't beat around the bush. She had adopted the professional, profiler look that turned him into a horny teenager. He wondered if he should tell his sister, the psychiatrist, about that. It was probably best that he keep his mouth shut. The last thing he needed was his sister asking him about his emotions and sex life.

"We understand he's being held somewhere so we can ask him a few questions?" Erica walked around the counter to the open door the deputy held for them.

"That's right," Owens answered. He motioned for them to follow him down the hall and stopped in front of a room with a glass window on the door. He unlocked the door, turned the handle, and pushed it open with his palm. Inside the room was a young man, probably in his early twenties, with a medium build and a pretty-boy face. He glowered at the three of them.

"I'm calling the mayor. When my father hears that you've kept me locked up without some kind of court order I'm going to sue your asses." Derek Holmes smirked. He sat back in his seat, shifting so his right arm draped over the chair's back.

"You haven't been locked up. Your father said you would cooperate. That's why you're here."

"Yeah, well making me sit in this little room waiting for you people is just as bad as holding me against my will."

Trent fisted his hands, ready to punch the little snot in the face for the way he was staring at Erica.

"And who are *you*?" Derek asked, his perverted little smile widening while he openly eyed Erica's body.

"I'm Agent Villa. This is Agent Buchanan." She pointed at Trent. "We need to ask you a few questions regarding some young women you dated recently."

Trent watched her move forward, until she stood across the table from where Derek sat. "We're investigating the deaths of Lisa Summers and Gina Torres."

"Yeah? I heard they were dead. What does that have to do with me?" He was still eyeing Erica's boobs with way too much interest. A snarl worked up Trent's throat. The wolf inside him wanted to come out, chew the little bastard and spit him out.

Trent focused on the job and not breaking the dumbass kid's jaw.

"I mean I went out with both of them. But after a while I got bored. Young girls get clingy, and I can't stand that." Derek winked at Erica.

Erica smiled, a cold little quirk of her lips that showed no amusement. She gripped the edge of the table. "Mr. Holmes, we've spoken to your father, and it was made clear to him that this is just a few questions. We can't hold you here without a formal charge if you don't want to be here, but we were told you'd be cooperating. I know your father doesn't want your family name dragged through the media in association with a murder case. We just need to ask you a few things. I understand this is not the place you would rather be."

She sounded almost apologetic, but then she pursed her lips, conveying she didn't really care how much they were bothering him. "But two girls are dead. Two girls *you* dated, Mr. Holmes. Now I suggest you cooperate with us, get yourself cleared, and then you can go back to your busy life."

"I've had nothing to do with them for months." He straightened.

She leaned forward, placed her hands palms flat on the table, and stared at him "Mr. Holmes." Her voice was soft, dripping ice. "I want to find whoever killed these girls. But I do not want to waste my time with someone who's innocent. Do you understand?"

"What is it you want to know?" he asked in a more serious tone of voice. Although his gaze was still stuck on Erica's rack, he appeared ready to cooperate. Trent had a hard time not walking up to Derek and bashing in his head.

Trent's heart took a nosedive when Erica outstretched her hand to shake the kid's.

She glanced at Trent for just a second, her eyes filled with frustration, before she turned back to Derek.

"I have a few questions. You are one of the few people both girls had in common. So where were you on the night both girls died, Mr. Holmes?"

"I already told your people that I was at a party both times." He shrugged. "What? I get invited to a lot of parties. I'm a popular guy."

"I understand that, Mr. Holmes. But you don't know who could have killed either girl?"

He shook his head. "I'm a busy guy. Once I'm done with them, I move on to bigger and better. They were kind of pissed at me when I broke things off, so I didn't bother staying friends."

"We also need to know if there is anyone you may know of who would want to hurt either Lisa or Gina."

Derek's smooth cockiness disappeared momentarily while he thought about her question. "I don't...wait. Gina mentioned a professor who made her feel kind of uncomfortable a time or two when she babysat for him. Some James Green.

"What about Lisa? Did she mention anyone to you?"

"Lisa had Green's class too at one point last semester, I remember because she gushed about him, but she never actually said she felt uncomfortable. He's the only one I remember both of them mentioning at one point or another."

"Mr. Holmes, thank you for your cooperation in this case. You're free to go. In the future, we'll direct any questions through your father's lawyer, who we've been told is your representative. But please, if you think of anything else that could be helpful to finding whoever killed these girls, give your sheriff's office a call or…" She pulled a card out of her pocket. "You can also call me."

"Oh, OK." Derek smiled, giving her what was clearly his most charming attempt at smooth and cool. "If you have any other questions you need to ask, you can call me directly. But only you." He winked at her.

After Derek Holmes walked out of the room, Trent watched Erica sit down and rub a hand over her forehead. She sighed. "He's not the one."

Well yeah, he'd known that much when the kid had told the truth, but still. Fuck. When she shook Holmes's hand and didn't freak out, he had known for sure. At least they had one suspect less.

NINE

Erica was still consumed by the strong emotions radiating off Derek Holmes. The kid was more than met the eye, but he was no killer. She saw and sensed that he liked adulation. But only a slight darkness surrounded him, which was minor compared to what she knew lived inside the person they were trying to find.

Her stomach churned painfully at the thought of another day without finding the murderer. He was intent on killing the college girls. Gulping at the knot in her throat, she followed Holmes outside. She looked at the sports car where Derek Holmes slid into the passenger side. He smiled at her before shutting the door. A strange sensation gripped her. She stopped and took a breath, but the air in her lungs evaporated, and the world went askew.

"What the fuck? Erica?" Trent sounded alarmed. He grabbed her by the arms just when her knees gave under her.

"I don't understand…" She continued to stare at the sports car.

The sun's glare didn't allow her to look inside the dark windshield. All she got was a glimpse of Holmes's smile. She panted, staring at the car as it made a turn, moving away from them and down the street. Could she have been wrong? Was Derek Holmes the killer? The dread that gripped her was one she'd experienced before, when she'd gotten close to a psychopath projecting his darkness outward. Evil could not be contained in some people. But she'd touched Derek and nothing had come across from the victims' deaths. So what in the world was going on?

It took her a moment to wade through her muddled mix of thoughts and emotions and realize that Trent was talking, asking her if she was all right. "Yes, I'm fine. Sorry, I got a little lightheaded for a moment."

Trent cupped her face, examining her for a minute before helping her into their Jeep. She tried to shut off into herself and dissect what happened, but he wouldn't be ignored.

"So what happened? I thought we established he wasn't our man?" He asked while he started the engine.

"I didn't think so, but when he got into his car I got such a strong connection for a moment there that I now wonder if I was wrong." She turned to look at his profile while he drove. "Which I can be, Trent. I *can* be wrong, and I might have just let a murderer go home."

He shook his head and grabbed her hand in his own, taking his eyes off the road for a second to watch her. "He's not the killer. He didn't lie to you at any point. We couldn't have kept him there anyway. We have no proof or evidence, but he is a person of interest. Although a group of girls said that he was with them so he's got an airtight alibi."

"But what if I—"

"Stop it. We can only work with what we know. As much as that kid seemed like the biggest jerk in this town, he didn't come across as a killer to me either." Trent squeezed her hand in his grasp, killing some of the panic growing inside her. "Take a deep breath, babe. We'll get him."

His reassurance melted the ice in her veins. He was right. They would catch that man. He rubbed circles over the top of her hand, each stroke decreasing her tension and increasing her desire to be held by him. Cursing her overactive hormones, she shifted in her seat, staring at his sexy face. She bit her lip. He had that scruffy beard that really turned her on and made her want to lick his face.

When she remembered how she'd woken up in his arms, feeling contented and safe, it once again made her heart jump to her throat. She was so fucked. Trent was quickly working his way past her shields and into territory where no one had ever ventured. How did he do that?

"Erica?" His question snapped her out of her thoughts.

"What?"

"I asked if he could have, like, mentally blocked you from seeing his true nature?" He gave her a sheepish grin. "I don't really know if he could do something like that, I'm just wondering."

She could tell it was strange for him to ask those questions, but he didn't back away. It made her like him even more for it.

She shook her head. "Honestly? I don't think he could. I've been doing this for a really long time. I put up shields to protect my thoughts from anyone tied to the victim. It would drive me insane to feel what each person emotionally linked to them is thinking or feeling when they come near me. I opened myself up when I shook his hand and didn't feel anything."

She laughed at Trent's look of disbelief.

"I don't mean the guy is an angel, but he's no murderer. If I'm correct, his worst crime is probably being too loud with some of his girlfriends. The murderer we're looking for is deeply connected to the victim, and I would feel the link when I meet the killer." She took a deep breath. "The best way I can explain it is: Killers are linked via energy to the person they killed. There's a darkness inside them that twines to the energy from the murder victim. When I see the killer, I can see the darkness. Even by just seeing or touching something of his, it would come through. That link between victim and murderer is established, and there's no breaking it."

He frowned, his eyes back on the road. "But then why did you react that way when he left?"

She shook her head. "I don't know, but it scares the shit out of me. I'm going to ask Brock to question him again. See what he gets from the kid."

There was no way she was going to take a chance at being wrong. She'd just opened her water bottle and taken a sip when her cell phone rang. Brock.

"Hi, Brock." Her gut fisted. Something told her

whatever he was going to say would not be good.

"We have another victim."

Shit.

"Melanie Lee. Same as the other girls. We're headed to the crime scene now, meet us there."

He rattled off the address.

"Do we know how long ago this one was killed?" She looked over at Trent. He glanced her way. His jaw clenched, and his hold on the wheel tightened to a white-knuckle grip.

"Not yet. She was found about an hour ago. The medical examiner is there now. I need you to look at her," he said. "There won't be any touching today, Erica. Do you understand?"

"I understand. We're on our way." She shut off the cell phone and gave Trent the address.

"What are you thinking?" he asked as they sped toward the crime scene.

"This isn't good." She bit her lip and frowned. "I have the feeling this man is playing with us. Dangling the bodies one after the other to see if we can figure it out."

"What do you think he knows that we don't?"

"I don't know, but I have a feeling what he knows is what will unlock this case."

She didn't like being played with. These were

human beings he'd killed, and she'd be damned if she allowed him to continue using those young women as toys in his sick game.

Brock and Ramirez were already at the crime scene when they arrived. Erica and Trent rushed out of the Jeep and darted past the police. Yellow tape and a few officers blocked off the entrance to the alley where they body had been dumped.

She stood transfixed, staring at the body of the young Asian woman. The urge to cry punched her in the chest. Her stomach turned. Bile rose as she scanned the mutilated torso. This girl had the same wounds on her naked body as the others but some extras over her face and neck. There were a lot more cuts and stab wounds on Melanie than on Gina. Lisa had only had the word carved into her stomach. Clearly the killer was getting into the swing of things and spreading his wings with each victim. Crouched down, she examined the girl's face in more detail, making sure not to touch anything. The scent of bleach drifted off the body when she lowered her head to study her wounds.

"Has the medical examiner arrived?" She jerked her face up when a pair of feet stopped by Melanie's head. It was Brock.

He pressed a button to end the call he'd been on.

"Yeah, the body is going to be moved to the hospital around the corner. I need information ASAP, and this is the closest location she can do an examination."

She nodded. Urgency ate at her. For every second they wasted, there was another life hanging in the balance. The killer wouldn't stop. He was having fun. She inspected the young girl's pale skin, dark hair, and bloody nails. Another fighter. It seemed that while his ultimate goal was to kill them, he got some kick out of hurting them. Sick bastard.

"Did you have any luck with the professor?" Trent asked.

Erica stood. Brock shook his head and grimaced down at the body in front of them. "We questioned him, but he mentioned that Gina was only his babysitter and admitted to having had an affair with Lisa. Once his wife found out they broke things off." He ran a hand through his short hair. "He mentioned Lisa wasn't very torn up about cutting things short. She always had a multitude of guys she dated."

"But what about his whereabouts during the approximate times of death? Did he have anything to say about that?" Erica strained to get the words out. She wanted to scream in frustration. This case was going nowhere.

"Actually, he has an airtight alibi. He's been

out of the country for almost four weeks, visiting family. He just returned two days ago. There's been a different professor doing his lectures in the meantime."

Great. Just what they needed, another dead-end.

She turned to Trent and caught him scrutinizing her. "Let's hope we have better luck with Richard Thompson and Anthony Holmes."

Trent's scowl intensified. She frowned, wondering what was wrong. She glanced at her hands, which was what he was staring at. That's when she realized he'd been studying her fisted hands. In order to calm down, she found the clenching and unclenching of her hands, combined with deep breathing techniques, helped her relax. At least that's what the paranormal unit psychiatrist had told her. So many victims in such a short span of time were playing havoc with her nerves. Just thinking of how much the victims had suffered made her angry.

Erica shifted from one foot to the other while the medical examiner went through the physical inspection of the body. Her hands itched to touch the victim, but with Trent on one side and Brock on the other, watching her like she might steal a body part, she decided to wait.

"Same as the others. This one died approximately three days ago," said the older woman looking at the body. The fiftyish, dark-haired medical examiner wore a white lab coat and gloves. She'd been recording the wounds, stating in a clear and concise manner all the traumas the victim had suffered.

"Was she reported missing?" Erica asked. The ME was poking around the body while they spoke.

"No," Brock replied. "From what we were told she'd scheduled to take ten days off, and no one had known she didn't make it to her family. Apparently they weren't expecting her for a few days anyway."

"So you're saying nobody knew that she had been missing?" Disbelief colored her words.

"I've got something here," the medical examiner said, calling their joint attention. In quiet suspense, they strode forward. She used a pair of long tweezers to pull out a piece of paper from the victim's throat. Erica held her breath. The ME unfolded the paper.

"What does it say?" Trent asked.

"She's not the last," the ME said, reading from the paper.

Erica's heart quaked. Blood froze in her veins, and a shudder racked her body. The killer wasn't stopping, but she already knew that.

"Give me the paper." She held her hand.

"No!" Both Brock and Trent yelled at once.

"Look…" She lowered her voice so that the ME wouldn't hear her. " I need to touch it to see if I can see him. We don't have time to waste."

She rushed around both men. Only a step away from grasping the tiny note, Trent wrapped his arm around her waist, hauling her back.

"Are you out of your mind, woman?" He dropped his head by her ear, his words a low murmur. "I know what you're trying to do. This is not the way to do it. We'll find something that belongs to the victim and see if you get any clue that way, but you're not touching something that was inside that dead girl's mouth. You know the rules. That is evidence and you can't contaminate it."

She wanted to argue, complain that they were running out of time, but what he said was the truth. Panic built inside her at breakneck speed.

"We should get this note analyzed by a handwriting expert." Brock's voice jerked her back to the present. "Villa, you and Buchanan question Richard Thompson. Go now. I will look into getting information on Anthony Holmes.

After you speak to him we'll go to Melanie Lee's dorm room." He gave Erica one of his do-not-argue-with-me looks. "We'll let you touch something of hers, but I want to be there. There's not going to be any more unnecessary risks to your health. Do you understand?"

She nodded, torn over having to wait. "When you visit Anthony Holmes, see Derek too. I don't know about him. I had a strange reaction when he was ready to leave."

Brock nodded. Trent followed her out of the building. God, she hoped she got something from Richard Thompson.

Trent marched to the Jeep beside her. Once inside she turned to look at him, knowing he'd been dying to say something. "OK, what is it?"

She thought he might be ready to yell at her over what she had almost done, and her hackles rose. But instead he cupped her face and kissed her on the lips.

"I know it's driving you crazy to see all these dead girls and not be able to figure out who did it." He slid his thumb over her jaw, back and forth. "Especially since you have to see what you do all the time, but you need to remember that in order to find this guy you have to stay ahead of him. You can't do something that will muddle your brain and stop you from thinking clearly. Or something that will jeopardize the case or the evidence."

Her heartbeat quickened to a loud gallop in her chest. He shifted, ready to sit back on his seat, when she gripped his T-shirt. She yanked him back toward her. Why she did it, she didn't know. She kissed him with all the pent-up desire she'd been feeling for him, with all the frustration she knew filled her brain. He just sat there and drank it all in. It was the most therapeutic kiss of her entire life.

Anger and frustration melted away with the soft swipes of his tongue over hers. His hands cupped her face and gently caressed her cheeks. The kiss went from hard and fast to slow and seductive in the blink of an eye. She sighed into the softer kiss. Emotions ran rampant inside her, unlocking doors that she'd never opened for any other man.

Trent propelled back, away from her. His features softened into a warm smile, a smile that spoke of a lot of things, all of which made it hard for her to swallow. But he didn't say any more, just sat back and started driving, leaving her to try and figure out what the hell she was going to do about him. Emotions were messy. Did she want to try? Was it possible he wanted something long-term? A soft sigh escaped her. She wouldn't dwell on that now there was a killer to catch.

They had just parked by Richard Thompson's apartment building when Erica's phone rang.

"Villa." She didn't recognize the number on the screen.

"Hey, it's Donovan."

Erica glanced at her phone's screen again. "This isn't your usual number, Donovan."

Her teammate laughed. "I know. I'm testing a new phone and decided to try it on you. Listen, I'm calling to tell you about Richard Thompson. Brock said you guys were going to interview him."

She glanced up at the five-story building. If she went by its appearance, Richard Thompson was another wealthy boy. "Yeah, we're outside his apartment building now."

"Ok, well you guys be careful. He's a known marijuana dealer and will most likely try to run if he thinks you're there to arrest him."

"Thanks for the heads up. I'll let Trent know, and we'll be on guard." She shut off the phone. Unsnapping her holster, she pulled out her gun. Trent did the same. "Thompson is a drug dealer, which is probably why everyone in the school is friends with him on Facebook." One tug on the door handle and she was able to hop out of the Jeep. Moments later Trent rushed around the vehicle, catching up with her before heading to the entrance, each gripping their weapons.

Trent nodded as they made their way into the building. "Makes sense. There's nobody that popular unless something else is in the mix." He grinned and winked at her. "At least, guys aren't usually that popular."

Opting for the stairs, since Thompson lived in the second level, they took note of the exits. When they reached Thompson's door, Erica pulled her tank top low, until it showed a major amount of cleavage. Then she knocked, arching her back to push her breasts out some more. She knew Trent watched her, so she smiled slyly at him and pursed her lips in an air kiss. A moment later the kid known as Thompson opened the door, and his gaze immediately dropped down to Erica's rack.

"Hi," she whispered, moving a foot to block the door from getting closed. But it was unnecessary; the kid's eyes were stuck on her breasts. "Are you Ricky?"

"Who's…ah, who's asking?" His eyes hadn't moved up from her boobs. She could have turned out to be a man, and he wouldn't have noticed. "My friend Melissa spoke about him to me." Her voice lowered. "She told me I could come see him, and he could get me something to help me relax." She hoped her voice sounded sexy enough.

Thompson opened the door a little wider to get a better look at her. Erica and Trent used that moment to hold the door open, though neither attempted to force their way into the apartment.

"Hey! What the—"

"You have two choices, kid. You talk to us now, or we can wait here and call the nice guys from Narcotics to come join in the party."

The kid let go of the door, his eyes darting all over the place as if ready to make a run for it.

Before he had a chance to move a muscle, Trent had him by the neck. He shoved him further into the apartment and down on a chair.

"What the hell do you want?" Thompson yelled, fighting Trent's grip. Unfortunately for him, Trent was big, strong, and unfazed by his escape attempts.

Trent snarled at Thompson. "Look, we have some questions. We're not here about your little operation. But like I said, if you prefer we can sit here and wait for Narcotics to come over and have a nice chat with you…"

The kid gave a quick shake of his head.

"I thought you'd see it my way. We need to know about some murder victims you were acquainted with. And we need to ask you some questions to see what you know and also rule you out as a suspect. Can you sit there without trying to leave?"

Thompson nodded and glanced up at Erica with big, frightened eyes. She stepped toward him, holding out her hand.

"I'm agent Villa, FBI." By the looks of him she knew he wasn't the killer, but she needed to make sure.

The kid hesitated for a moment, but Trent's gun still pointing his way must have intimidated him enough to move. Thompson lifted a shaky hand and enveloped hers. Other than the kid having a very cold skin, there was nothing. Absolutely nothing. She wanted to yell in frustration.

"Did you know Lisa Summers, Gina Torres, and Melanie Lee?" She sat across from Thompson.

Thompson gulped. It shocked her to see that the popular dealer resembled a snotty little kid. If he was one hundred pounds she'd be shocked.

"How old was he?" She didn't realize she'd asked the question out loud until he answered.

"I'm seventeen."

Her disbelief must've shown because he continued. "I'm in an early college program."

"So let me get this straight. You're a smart kid. Really smart from the looks of it. You get into college much earlier than most people, and you decide to ruin your chances of succeeding by selling weed?" Trent growled.

Thompson rolled his eyes. "Yeah, well not everyone is a chick magnet or Mr. Popularity. I did what I had to. You don't know what it's like to have to worry about everyone wanting to pick on you if you don't have something going for you. I wasn't going to be the kid everyone picked on in high school and then in college too."

Trent clenched his jaw and appeared ready to argue with the boy, but Erica stopped him with her question. "Did you know those girls?"

Thompson glanced down at his lap, folding and unfolding his thin fingers. "Yes."

"How did you know them?" She prodded.

The boy's skin had turned a deep shade of red from either embarrassment or anger. She'd guess embarrassment from the way his reedy frame shook. His T-shirt looked two sizes too big, and his glasses overwhelmed his small face. She almost felt bad for him. Almost.

Thompson gulped, lifted his head, and gaped at Erica, fear clear in his gaze. "I sold a guy they dated some stuff. Derek Holmes. He always came with a different girl."

Always back to Holmes. "What about other guys, did you see any of them with anyone else?"

Richard shook his head. "Sometimes Derek and the girls came with his brother, but mostly it was just him and whoever he was dating."

Erica's frustration had to have shown on her face, because Trent moved beside her, grabbed her hand, and held it for a moment. She turned to him, but he was focused on Thompson.

Trent sighed. "Look kid, I know fitting in is hard."

Thompson curled his lip, his eyes filled with disbelief.

"Yeah, I do know. When I was your age I looked just like you, probably worse since I had four older sisters who tried to make me look like their version of cool. But then I hit a growth spurt, and I filled out. The thing is you can't lower your standards just to make friends. You lose part of yourself if you do."

Erica stood, and they strolled to the door. She stopped just shy of the threshold and turned to the boy. "We're not going arrest you…this time. But if you don't want to be reported and kicked out of this school, you will get rid of whatever merchandise you have and stop the sales," she ordered, her tone firm. "I'm coming back to check on you, and I'm not giving you advance notice."

Thompson darted over to his desk drawer, pulled out a plastic bag filled with his product, and ran back to them. He handed the bag over to Trent.

"Don't worry," he said, glancing from Trent to Erica. "I'm done. It was giving me ulcers to sell that stuff anyway. I was always worried I'd get found out."

To drive home the importance of what he had done, Erica lifted a brow, wiping any and all concern from her features. "You're lucky I'm in a good mood. Normally I'd have kicked your ass, arrested you, and then told your parents. I hope you don't give me a reason to still do that."

Thompson's pale face got a shade lighter, and he hunched in on himself.

She was of the belief that sometimes you needed to scare the crap out of some people for them to realize the dumb shit they were doing.

Outside the building Trent grabbed her by the waist and kissed her. "What was that for?"

"You're so hot when you get bitchy." He grinned and kissed her again.

It took a moment for her to absorb what he'd said. When she did she growled at him. "Asshole."

He chuckled. "No baby, I prefer pussy, but if you really want to try I'll give it a go."

She couldn't stay angry when he always came back with some sexual response. He was incorrigible.

While they drove, her mind focused on what was left. She needed to touch something of Melanie Lee's, and she hoped to be able to see more than with the previous two victims. Things were moving too slow for her liking. To top it off, she now had Trent and how he made her feel to worry about. Life didn't seem to get any simpler for her.

"Stop thinking so hard." He squeezed her hand over her lap. She glanced his way and caught him smiling. "I can see your brain trying to figure out how to handle me."

The nerve of the man. OK, so maybe that's exactly what she'd been doing, but he didn't need to point it out. "Yeah? And what do you suggest I do?"

"Just go with the flow." He grinned and went back to focusing on the road. He was right. She'd have to wait and see what he was about before she stopped having sex with him.

By the time they finished their visit with Thompson it was late. Erica was tired and hungry, and she could only assume Trent was too. Her phone rang just as she contemplated stopping for a bite to eat.

"Hi, Brock."

"Villa. Everything OK?"

She sighed. "All is still the same."

Silence met her words. "I want you both back here. We'll debrief and see where we stand. It's late anyway."

When they got there, Donovan was setting food on the table.

"Don't worry, I didn't cook," she joked. Everyone in the department knew Donovan couldn't cook worth a damn. She'd tried to bring things when they had potlucks but her food always went uneaten. She was such a good sport she'd never taken offense but continued to try whenever the opportunity presented itself. The woman was certainly persistent. Too bad she sucked at it.

"So if you're not poisoning us, er...I mean if you didn't make this, where did it come from?" Trent grinned and grabbed a biscuit.

Donovan slapped his other hand when he went for a piece of chicken. "Remember the lady you guys went to visit, where Gina Torres lived?"

"Ms. Lipkin?" Erica laughed when Ramirez went to grab a roll, only to get smacked much harder than necessary by Jane.

"Yeah. She sent a bunch of food and said 'she

couldn't have those two handsome young men starving.'" Donovan slapped Ramirez again when he made a second attempt. He pouted like a sulking kid, which made both women laugh.

"Jesus. What is it with you women and violence?" Ramirez complained and sat down, waiting for everyone so they could eat.

"Tell me about it, bro. I'm gonna have to teach Erica to relax or sleep with one eye open. She's vicious I tell you." He then dodged a balled napkin Erica threw at him. "See what I mean?"

"Whatever happened to loving and obeying your man?" Ramirez asked, shaking his head.

Erica lifted her brows and glared at Trent. "Whatever happened to shutting your mouth for self-preservation? I thought you wanted to live well into old age? Keep talking."

"Sweetheart, you know that was all Ramirez," Trent said and shrugged at Ramirez's outraged gasp. "Sorry man, but you know how it is. She's got the goods so she's in charge." He used his serious voice.

Erica and Donovan burst into giggles. One thing was for sure, if she decided to try a relationship with Trent, she'd never be bored.

TEN

Trent winked at Erica and blew her a kiss. Brock chose that moment to walk into the room. "What's going on?"

He joined them at the table.

"Not much. Trent was just teaching Ramirez how women rule because they have the goods." Donovan snickered and piled food on her plate.

Trent's heart soared when Erica grinned at him. He didn't care how stupid he had to act in order to keep that smile on her face. Now all he needed to do was get her alone and tell her about his not-exactly-human status.

"So what did you find out with Anthony Holmes?" Erica asked Brock while they passed food around the table.

"There was no chance to speak to the kid. Apparently he's been in some kind of retreat and won't be back until tomorrow." Brock took a bite of chicken and hummed. "Jesus. Who made this? And can we hire her for however long we're here?"

Trent was in agreement. Ms. Lipkin might be an older woman, but she sure knew her way around a kitchen.

"So that's it? We have to wait? What if someone else dies in the meantime?" Erica's voice hitched. "Do we just let the bodies pile one on top of the other? I have to…no, I need to figure this out."

She sat rigid in the chair, frowning at her plate.

Trent heard the words she didn't say. That it was going drive her crazy to keep seeing those deaths and not put whoever did it behind bars. The scent of her frustration and fear mingled and made his animal pace inside him.

"We all want to stop whoever this killer is, Villa," Ramirez added.

Erica turned to Donovan. "Have there been any finger print matches from the first two victims to anyone on the Integrated Automated Fingerprint Identification System?"

Donovan shook her head and sipped her tea.

"Whoever did this isn't in IAFIS. If we can get a definite lead on someone, we could get more prints tested. Some prints were pulled Gina's body, but none of the ones from Lisa were prints we could use."

"And have we gotten anything we can use from Gina?" Her voice was soft yet demanding.

"No. We did get some DNA samples to put through CODIS from Gina. Even with a rush, the lab takes seventy-two hours to get a DNA code, and then it takes at least twenty-four more hours to put that through our system." Donovan sighed. "If we go by that we won't be looking at results until another two to three days at the minimum."

Trent eyed Erica. She clenched and released her fists on her lap, next to him. He wiped his hands on a napkin and curled his fingers over hers. Satisfaction spread through him when she leaned closer and opened her hand so that he could link their fingers together.

"When the other Holmes kid shows up you question him, Villa," Brock knew as much as Trent that she had to see both of the Holmes boys. "Thankfully the father's lawyer said he'd get the kid to come meet with us as soon as he returns."

The rest of the meal passed in a blur, and soon they were headed to their rooms. Trent had a feeling Erica would try to shut him out again, so he took the lead and waited for her by the door to her bedroom.

"Trent…" She sighed. "What are you doing?"

"Let's go to bed, love." He tugged her into the room and shut the door.

There was confusion and vulnerability in her eyes. He held her in his arms and kissed her. Her hands crawled up to his shoulders, stroking him over his T-shirt. She dug her nails into his biceps while rubbing her body over his. Using sex to convince her into a relationship would never work, but he hoped it would at least soften her up enough to allow her to consider it.

"Trent—"

"Shhh. Stop thinking so hard, sweetheart. It's time to relax your mind."

He undressed her and himself. They made their way into the bathroom. They kissed in the tub while water ran over their bodies. Trent used the loofah to wash Erica, sliding the soft spongy material over her curves. Afterward she took it out his hand to return the favor. She ran her hands down his body, tracing his muscles, until she reached his cock. Arousal electrified his brain cells and powered down his veins. His breath caught in his lungs. He was hungry for a taste of her. She jerked him in her hand, squeezing him from root to tip. He groaned, his vision fixating on her, staring at her pink tongue twirling circles over his nipple. Her hold on his cock tightened into a perfect grip.

"Oh... Jesus."

She got down on her knees and sucked his cock into her hot mouth, sliding his entire length between her pouty lips. He pulled the wet strands from her face and thrust into the slick cavern of her mouth. She jerked, sucked, and ran her tongue over him like he was a tasty piece of candy and she had a craving for sugar.

After a few minutes of enjoying her lavishing pleasure on his cock, he grabbed her by the arms and tugged her off him.

"Hey!"

"I love how you suck my cock, but I really want to fuck you now."

"*Si*, please." She moaned and curled one leg around his hip. "I need you."

He palmed her ass cheeks and lifted her up until both her legs went around his waist. She held on to his neck and started kissing him with so much desperation and passion he almost lost sight of what he was supposed to be doing. He lowered her onto his cock, gliding her body down, her pussy sucking his cock on its descent. Their gazes locked. Her eyes were filled with passionate need.

"Fuck me." She moaned into his lips.

He slammed his back against the tiled wall, the move shoving his cock deeper into her.

She whimpered. "*Oh.* That feels so good."

Trent lifted and dropped her on his cock repeatedly, her muscles clenching on every slide down, heightening his pleasure. Her nails dug into his shoulders, her teeth nipped at his jaw, and her breasts rubbed on his chest. He squeezed her ass and rocked her on his cock. She groaned, licked his neck, and sucked on his lip.

"So good…Harder!"

He groaned and chuckled. Even in the middle of sex she couldn't stop being bossy. God, he really must be in love, because there could be no other reason for him to find that cute.

Holding her firmly by her ass, he continued to lift and drop her. She moaned, groaned, wiggled her hips, and begged him for more. He increased speed, and she sighed and dropped butterfly kisses on his neck in approval.

"Yes…Fuck. I'm so close. So close..." Her breath hitched. Her pussy fluttered, and her muscles squeezed his cock. She bit her lip and moaned, shaking and arching into him as she climaxed.

The tight grip her body had over his shaft sent him over the edge. His orgasm shot down his spine, lighting nerve endings and sparking fires in his brain, until it gathered at his cock. His balls drew tight. He shivered and growled into her shoulder when he came. They panted and stared at each other for a moment. Something other than lust shone in her eyes. He lowered her legs to the tub floor, cupped her face, and kissed her.

He pulled a fluffy towel off a shelf and dried her off first and himself after. When she held his hand on their way to bed, his smile could not be contained. But when she curled into his side on the bed, searching for his touch, he knew that they were moving in the right direction.

Once they were settled comfortably on the bed, he was surprised when she brought up the subject he'd been afraid to speak of.

"So what do you do that makes you interesting enough to be on this unit. Are you psychic or something?" Her soft words made his nerves rise.

"No. My ability is different than yours."

She glanced up at him, her eyes filled with curiosity, and smiled. "Well what is it? You know my deep dark secret. Or don't you trust me?"

"God, no! That's not it at all. It's just that...I'm a little concerned with what you'll think."

The corners of her eyes crinkled. "Trust me, I'm the last person to judge, but you don't have to tell me if you don't want to."

He scented her concern, and it made the

decision for him. "I'm a shifter."

She frowned. "A what?"

He gulped. His wolf paced inside him, worried over what his mate would think. "I can shift from man to animal."

Her eyes went saucer-wide. "Y-you…you can?"

He nodded, his heart pounding so loud in his ears he could hardly hear her words.

"What, um, what animal can you shift into?"

"A wolf."

He waited, watching her for any signs of disgust, fear, or dislike. After a moment her smile grew wider.

"That is…amazing. I wish I could do something that cool."

He laughed. He couldn't believe how well she'd taken it. Tugging her up for a kiss, he hugged her tight and grinned. "It is pretty cool."

"Will you show me?" She licked her lips and caressed a finger over his jaw. "Not now, but when we're somewhere that's easy for you to shift?"

"I promise to show you soon. Real soon."

"This is great. Much better than me thinking you were some kind of psychic or a witch." She yawned.

"No witch here, just a wolf."

"My wolf." Her words were heavy with sleep, but they filled his heart with joy. She didn't realize just how right she was. *He was her wolf*, he thought as he let sleep claim him.

A soft whimper woke him from sleep. He turned to look at Erica who was curled away from him in the fetal position. Slowly, he turned her, pulling her into his arms. She shifted and ended up draped over him, hugging his upper body, her arms going around his torso.

"Make it stop," she mumbled low, voice thick with sleep and tears.

He peeked down at her face, but she was still asleep.

"Shhh, my love. It's alright. I'm here with you. I'll never leave you." He promised. It was a while later, and a lot of comforting words and caresses from him, before Erica finally fell into a quiet sleep.

He was more determined than ever to prove to her he was the right man for her, because he knew that she was definitely the right woman for him and his wolf.

The following morning found the group

headed back to the college. Brock drove his vehicle along with Rodriguez. Trent, Erica, and Donovan took the Jeep. It had been decided early on that they would move in on this quickly. Neither Brock nor Erica wanted to wait around for a new body to appear. So they were going in to search Melanie's room as a group. When they reached the campus housing for Melanie Lee, they parked outside the victim's building.

Erica observed while Brock opened the door to Melanie's dorm room. He held it open for her to walk in ahead of everyone. She didn't touch anything at first. Her gaze scanned the room for anything that might help the investigation. Framed photos lined the walls. One in particular caught Erica's attention.

It was the same as Gina Torres. Melanie was dressed in costume with a masqueraded man to either side and two other men at her back. One had his mask askew: Derek Holmes. She couldn't make out the other man's face under his mask. She frowned and stared at Derek Holmes. The same sick, twisting sensation she'd had when he'd gotten into his car had returned.

"I really need to see Derek Holmes again. I know there's something I'm missing with that kid." She said. When she turned, everyone stared at her, all watching her quietly. None of them gave her any strange looks, more like expectant, waiting to see if she could come up with something.

Brock nodded. "You got it. I'm going to get you in to see both brothers today."

Erica strolled up to Melanie's bed. Pink and purple covered most of the surfaces on everything in the small room, as well as the bedding and decorations. It was so perfectly organized it would make any anal-retentive person proud.

She took a breath, noting that Trent stood right beside her, while Brock and the others waited further back.

"Erica?" Brock's voice stopped her before she grabbed the blanket.

She turned to face her boss and friend. He never called her by her given name in front of anyone else. "I've filled Jane and Tony in on your special ability and the need to keep it under wraps at all times."

Tony and Jane nodded, both their faces showed nothing but concern. "We've got your back, E," Tony vowed.

"All the time," Jane added.

Her heart constricted. For so long she'd been made to feel inadequate because of what she did, what she saw. Now the people that could make her life more difficult were letting her know nothing had changed. She'd have to talk to Brock about outing her. Even if he felt it necessary, he should have consulted her first. Trent's warmth radiated toward her.

"I'm right here, sweetheart."

Her wolf. He made her feel so protected. It was easier to delve into the darkness of evil with him by her side. More determined than ever to find the killer, she took another breath and grabbed hold of the pink and purple blanket.

Melanie peered around her, trying to make sense of what was going on. A searing pain took hold of her stomach. It was hard to focus, but she tried by blinking several times. She was tied to a reclining seat. The musky scent of rain or water drifted all around her, but she still didn't know where she was. There wasn't any loud, pulsing music this time. Nothing to help her figure out where Melanie was.

She glanced around in a hazy circle. Melanie had been drugged as well. She peeked down at her stomach. He'd already cut the words into her. The figure wearing a dark hood approached her from the shadows. His face was completely unidentifiable in the badly lit room.

"You shouldn't have rejected me," he whispered in a deep angry hiss. "I'm better than him."

Melanie's screams of pain while he stabbed her made it hard for Erica to hold on to the scene. When she opened her eyes she was on Trent's lap in the Jeep.

Brock sat in the front passenger side looking back at her, while Tony took the driver's seat.

Trent caressed her face. "How are you doing?"

She shook her head and leaned into him. "Not good. I got nothing. Nothing we didn't have before. Where are we going?"

She finally realized the vehicle was moving.

"We got word a new girl has gone missing. We're going to her house now." Brock's grim face made her stomach knot. Another girl. She'd had a feeling the killer would step up his game. Now here she was, with a new missing person and no leads. She needed to see Derek Holmes again.

"Brock I really think Derek Holmes might have something to do with this. I want to see him right away." She sounded frantic even to her own ears, but she wouldn't let this new girl die.

Brock nodded. "We'll go see the new missing girl's family. See what we can gather from them, and then you and Trent can head to the Holmes household. We'll see about gathering information on this girl."

"What's her name?" Erica's vision blurred. She rubbed a hand over her forehead; a migraine was taking hold.

"Casey Young." Brock replied just as they reached a large Victorian home nestled in a quiet and affluent neighborhood. The houses looked like they'd been pulled out of a *House and Garden* magazine.

Police officers greeted them at the door, along with a very concerned set of parents. Erica addressed the mother. "Where's Casey's room?"

The woman didn't question Erica's abrupt tone of voice, just guided her to the girl's bedroom. She opened the door and pointed Erica inside. "This is Casey's room. No one comes in here so everything is exactly as she left it yesterday."

Trent and Brock followed behind her. Trent made his way to her side. "What do you think you're doing?"

"We're out of time, Trent. I need to see." She glanced up at the mirror. A picture, just like the one in Melanie and Gina's rooms sat there. Casey was dressed in costume and an unmasked Derek Holmes stood to one side, hugging her. Two other men were at her back. To her other side was a different guy in a mask. Had all the girls attended the same party? She stared at the man to her right and was caught by something about him. There. His arm was draped over Casey's shoulder, the move showed off a pentagram tattoo on the top of his hand.

"What are you staring at?" Brock asked.

"Remember how I mentioned these photos with the masked men? We need to see if we can find out who these guys are. Clearly one of them is Derek Holmes. The other victims also had photos like this. Who knows if one of the other three is our man?" She continued eyeing the man's hand. She remembered seeing the same tattoo on the man in both Melanie and Gina's photos. Clearly the guy was the same throughout. She wondered who he was.

"Get the full story from the cops. I'll stay here with her." Brock said.

Trent hesitated, but after a moment left to follow Brock's orders.

Something about the photograph made Erica grab hold of it.

She gasped, immediately surrounded by darkness. Casey's eyes had been blindfolded, the girl couldn't see anything, and because of that neither could Erica.

"They're not going to find you. Don't worry doll, I won't kill you for a few days. I'm going to have some fun with you first," a deep voice whispered by her ear.

Casey's heart beat so loud it was almost impossible for Erica to make out what the man said. Casey mumbled over the gag in her mouth.

"No. You had your chance. I wanted you more than the others. They were all whores, but you, you were smarter, better. I knew we could work well. But you still chose to reject me in favor of a womanizing dog. You need to get hurt. It will teach you about turning me down."

Erica was pulled from the conversation when someone called out to her.

"Erica?" Brock carried her this time.

"What happened? Why'd you pull me back?" she growled.

Anger overran every thought. She'd been so close. If only she had heard more, she might know where he had her. Already she knew it was possible Casey wasn't dead. Which meant she needed to find her. Right. Now. Erica wiggled in Brock's grasp, wanting to be let down.

"Stop it." He sighed. "You started shaking and breathing shallow. We couldn't just leave you like that."

"Where's Trent?" she asked, needing him close now that she was tired and scared for Casey. He was the only person she wanted to see.

"He'll be out in a moment. He and Tony are still gathering details from the police while Jane speaks to the parents." Brock set her down in front of the Jeep and opened the door for her to sit in the front passenger side.

She looked Brock straight in the eyes. "She's alive, Brock. And I need to speak to Derek Holmes. He's linked to this somehow. I don't know why I didn't see it when I met him, but it was there when I touched that photo."

"Fine. You and Trent can go ahead to the

Holmes residence. We'll continue gathering information here."

Trent jogged toward them. Seeing him made her feel better instantly.

ELEVEN

"So why are we going back to the Holmes household?" Trent took his eyes off the road to quickly glance at Erica. She had her hands clasped tightly in her lap, and a deep frown covered her face. Fear came off her in waves, spiking his own anxiety over her safety.

"I need to see Derek Holmes again. Everything leads back to him somehow, and I don't know why I couldn't feel it when I touched him. He's not that mentally strong, and no true evil came through before. But I'm not perfect. So maybe this is one of those times we can't depend of my sight."

"Let's do it the old-fashioned way then. Derek

Holmes knew each of these victims, including Casey Young. They've all dated him and had some connection to him. It seems to me he is our most likely suspect."

He gazed at Erica again and saw her shake her head and bite her lip. "It's not that simple. Derek Holmes is a Casanova. He thrives on female attention. I just don't see him that worried about a couple of girls *he* dumped. From what we know he's the one that cut each of these girls off for the next one. So why would he want to kill them after? It just doesn't make any sense."

Trent pulled into a long private driveway. At the end of the circular drive stood an imposing, Victorian-style mansion. The Holmeses had a lot of money. And a lot of high-powered connections.

Erica jumped out of the Jeep before he had a chance to completely stop the car. Her ponytail swung down her back when she jogged toward the front door. As he got to her side, the front door opened from inside.

A tall, older man dressed in a gray butler suit eyed both of them with interest. "May I help you?"

Trent pulled out his identification. "Yes, we're here to speak to Derek and Anthony Holmes."

The man's brows lifted but said nothing for a

moment. "Neither the younger nor older Holmes are present at this time."

"Well where are they?" Erica's stepped forward, crowding the butler.

The butler frowned at Erica's aggravated tone but answered her question. "Derek is at the country club with friends and Anthony may or may not be at his cabin."

"Do you mind if we come inside and look around a little?"

The butler gave him a stiff nod. "Not at all. Mr. and Mrs. Holmes indicated you would be stopping by and to allow you to look around and answer any questions if necessary."

Trent followed behind Erica into the large receiving area. He watched her immediately regard everything, searching for a clue or something to help guide her in understanding what Derek Holmes was about.

Unfortunately, that area of the house was like a hotel room, completely impersonal. Trent sensed her frustration rising. She'd fisted her hands tightly to her sides. They moved down a corridor to the next open space. A family room.

A large portrait of the family, hanging over the fireplace, caught Erica's attention. She stopped mid-step and stared.

Trent stepped up beside her, wondering what

it was about the photo that made her lose all color to her face. He whispered near her ear. "What is it?"

Erica turned a horrified face toward him "That's the second man in the photos with the victims." She whispered and glanced at the butler, who had been following quietly behind them. Her voice shook, and she pointed to the family portrait. "Who is he?"

The butler moved up beside them. "The photo is Mr. and Mrs. Holmes and their sons."

Erica shook her head. "Who's the man in the back, right side?"

Trent eyed the man in question. He was a young man. Probably nineteen or twenty with dark eyes and a large build. A handsome guy, just like Derek Holmes. The rigid set of his features made him look angry and arrogant, but nothing that would make him suspect the kid to be a murderer. He had a hand draped over Mrs. Holmes' shoulder. The strange pentagram tattoo on his hand caught Trent's attention. It wasn't what one usually displayed on a family portrait. Erica's reaction gave Trent the feeling they'd found their killer.

"That's Anthony," the butler replied.

Erica's face turned an ashier shade of gray. "I need to see his room."

Trent held her cold hand while they followed the butler to the second level, where the bedrooms were located. Every time they went past a portrait that included Anthony Holmes, Erica stopped and stared at his eyes for a few moments, until he had to drag her from the picture. Her reaction worried him.

When they reached the open door to Anthony Holmes' room, Erica rushed into the bedroom. Trent's heart slowed to a crawl when he realized what she was going to do.

"Erica, don't do anything just yet," he yelled and darted after her.

She stood in the middle of the bedroom and turned in a full circle. Trent stared at her for a moment, to make sure she wouldn't just grab something, before he glanced around the room. It was not what he'd expected after what they'd seen of the rest of the house. The bedroom was painted a dark gray, almost black, color.

Skulls and all kinds of demonic photography covered the walls. The bed was covered in a black bedspread. Black panels covered the windows, and if the light hadn't been on it would've been pitch black inside the room. Erica contemplated the night tables beside the bed. Small figures of horned angels with large fangs and red, beady eyes sat on the surface. Anthony Holmes might be into the gothic scene, but that didn't make him a killer.

She marched over to a door. He ran over to where she stood, ready to grab a knob and stopped her.

"Let me do it."

Grasping the knob and twisting, he opened what he'd assumed was a closet door. When they looked inside, they saw hell.

Trent's gut clenched and turned to Erica. "What made you want to look in here?"

Her features were set in such a sad expression it made him want to reach out to her. "Evil calls out to me."

The room was small, probably a closet of some sort, but it was packed with vital information on their case. Photos of all the victims while suffering different levels of torture were taped haphazardly on the walls. Gina's bloody face with her mouth open in a scream of agony made Trent's stomach tighten. Lisa's pleading look in another ratcheted up his growing anger.

Photos of Melanie Lee, crying, screaming, and, finally, dead were mixed in with the others. Bloody photos of Anthony's carvings on their bodies and remains were all over. Trent couldn't wait to get his hands of the sadistic bastard.

Locks of hair and pieces of clothing sat on a small table inside the closet. How had no one noticed that before?

"We need to find him. Right now." Erica was panicked. Trent turned to look at her, but she grabbed hold of his shirt and gripped the material in her fists. "He has Casey Young. I don't know how long he'll keep her alive. He said a few days, but what if he changes his mind?" She tightened her hold on the shirt. "We have to go. Now."

He nodded, in complete agreement with her. They moved back, stepping away from Anthony Holmes's personal victim collection.

Trent glanced back to the butler standing by the room entrance. "Where is Anthony Holmes now?"

The butler, finally showing emotion, stood there with his eyes wide, in total shock. He gawked at the still open closet for a moment before responding. "I-I believe he's at his cabin at this time."

"Where's this cabin? We need to go there now," Trent said.

The butler gave him instructions on reaching the other end of the property where Anthony Holmes kept a cabin by the river.

Erica ran to the Jeep. Air fought its way into her lungs, and her mind filled with images of Casey Young. She had to get to her before

Anthony killed her. The evil radiating from his room and his possessions, including his photos, made it hard for her to think straight.

"Wait! Erica, wait," Trent yelled.

She turned to him just as she was about to slide into her seat.

He ran to the trunk, moments later he rushed back to her side and brought her a bulletproof vest.

"Trent we need to go."

"Put it on," he ordered. "I'm not taking any chances with your life! Besides, you know the rules. You can't go into a dangerous location without one of these."

"Don't you need one too?" Her concern for him grew when she realized he didn't plan on putting a vest on.

"No. It doesn't help me if I need to shift."

"But what if you get hurt?"

He cupped her face for a moment and glanced deep into her eyes. "I'll be fine."

She put her vest over her tank top and sat in the passenger seat, waiting for Trent to take them to the cabin and hoping they found Casey alive.

Anthony Holmes had Casey Young in the cabin by the river. She was sure of it. It explained the water and the isolation, why no one ever heard the screams. Now she understood why she kept thinking Derek Holmes was the culprit. He was in the photos with Anthony and the victims. Erica couldn't discern who was radiating the evil, she just saw Derek.

Her ass bumped in the seat as Trent drove through the rough terrain to get to the other side of the property. They went through a rocky section that made Erica hang on to the door to keep from flying out the window. She didn't care if she ended up bruised all over; she just wanted to reach Casey Young while she was still alive.

The Jeep swerved over a bunch of dead branches, creating a loud cracking noise. When they passed a bend, they finally saw the cabin, a one-story building that was clearly meant as a retreat. All the windows were covered, and no noise sounded from anywhere. Erica's stomach twisted in knots. What if he already killed and disposed of Casey?

She jumped out of the Jeep and drew her gun. Although nervous inside, her hand was rock steady when she neared the cabin. One thing she was good at was shooting. Trent also held out his weapon. She gave him a hand signal: she'd take the back door and he would use the front. Erica didn't want to chance losing Anthony.

Trent headed to the front of the cabin. Quietly,

she made her way around the side, taking in the covered windows. She reached the back door in moments and tried the knob. It was open, which she found strange, but knew Anthony probably thought he wouldn't be found.

Goosebumps broke out on her skin. She traveled the kitchen area in silence. Her trainers allowed her to move stealthily in the space. Large knives and other surgical equipment had been placed on the kitchen counter. Not a single dish, cup, or food item could be seen.

Upon reaching a small door, she turned the knob to check the inside. More knives were sitting on the shelves of the pantry area. Erica stepped back, moved down the hall, and neared a larger door.

The room was dark due to the window coverings, but she was still able to see. A bed with chains and belts tied to the posts was located to the right. Erica's attention was caught by a portable closet. She opened the door and came face to face with a wide-eyed, bound, and very scared Casey Young. A still-alive Casey.

Erica lifted her badge from her chest to show the girl she was there to help. Then she placed a finger to her lips and motioned Casey to stay quiet. Casey nodded sharply. Erica heard a squeaking noise from behind her and turned around to point her gun at the entrance. She didn't see anything, but her instincts told her someone was near. The girl was battered and bleeding, with duct tape covering her lips. Her hands were bound behind her back, and her feet were tied.

Erica reached into her pocket for a blade. Keeping her vision focused on the door, she cut the bindings from Casey's feet. She helped Casey take a few steps until she reached the bed. Casey's weight leaned into Erica's side. She just wanted to get the girl out of that cabin. It took painstaking minutes to help Casey cut the rope binding her hands behind her back. Erica winced when Casey pulled off the duct tape from her lips, leaving her lips broken and bleeding. The girl stood on shaky legs but walked behind Erica toward the kitchen.

They were a few yards away from the back door when the kitchen door opened. A man held a gun in his hand, his face twisted in rage. Anthony.

"Run!" She turned and shoved Casey backward to the safety of the hallway.

Anthony lifted his gun and pointed it at Erica.

"You can't have her. She's mine!" he yelled as Erica lifted her own weapon.

A loud, piercing growl made Anthony's attention snap to the other side of the kitchen. A huge white wolf bared his teeth and rushed toward them. Anthony fired at the large wolf.

"No!" Erica screamed and fired at Anthony. The animal leaped through the air and took Anthony down with his massive body. Anthony screamed and shot blindly at the wolf. Loud snarls and growls filled the air. She couldn't shoot again for fear of hitting the wolf. Erica watched in horror as Anthony was mauled by the wolf. More shots rang out, over and over.

"Trent!"

The wolf continued to maul the man until all that was left was a bloody mess. Anthony's lifeless body lay on the ground surrounded by a pool of blood. The wolf moved toward her, took a few steps, stopped, and fell to his side.

She rushed forward, dropping to the ground next the large furry body. "Trent?"

His body contorted, and his bones popped. The wolf howled. It looked so painful she glanced away. The sound of cracking bones became hard for her to hear, making her nauseated. When it stopped she peeked back at a naked, bleeding Trent.

"Oh god. Tell me what to do. Tell me how to help you, please!"

Her heart stopped beating when she saw the gunshot wounds.

He panted and groaned. "I'll be ok. Just need

to shift back."

"Why did you shift to human in the first place?"

"Because… I had to tell you…Erica…I love you."

"Shift dammit! Go back to your furry-tailed body and fix yourself. Please," she demanded in a panic, her voice hoarse. Her heartbeat thundered wildly in her chest.

His bones twisted, making that painful-sounding noise. A knot formed in her throat, expanding along with the fear filling her veins.

"You'll be ok, Trent."

She dialed Brock, all the while putting pressure on the wounds she saw bleeding. Fear mounted inside her, and tears dripped down her cheeks, but she refused to believe he would be anything other than ok. She laid her head over his furry chest to listen to his heartbeat. He could not just tell her he loved her and die. She wouldn't let him.

TWELVE

Erica contemplated Trent while he slept. She didn't want to risk him waking and finding her there, so she left after checking his vitals and speaking to his doctor. Apparently shifters were quick at healing, but Trent was shot so many times it took longer for him to heal. Brock brought him into a specialized area of a government hospital to let him continue his recuperation.

It was still hard for her to remember the sounds of the shooting. There had been ten shots in all. His body pushed most of the bullets out, but some had to be removed by doctors. She'd been amazed that after two days he was almost back to fully operational. His wounds, wounds that would've killed any other man, had only delayed his healing. Visiting him while he slept allowed her to check his progress and gave her the chance to watch him heal without him actually knowing she was there. If he knew she was there, she was afraid he'd start questioning her on the future of their relationship, a relationship she wasn't sure really existed.

It didn't matter that she didn't do relationships; she still had feelings, deep ones, for Trent. But she knew that what they'd shared in New York had been something that wouldn't last. He was a ladies' man, and while she'd wanted to, she wasn't sure she could figure out how to make a relationship work.

It was her last time visiting Trent. She knew he'd be released in a few days and didn't want to chance him finding her in his hospital room.

Outside his door she bumped into Brock.

"Erica." He grabbed her before she stepped back and hit the doorframe. She glanced up and caught him frowning at her. "Where are you going?"

"Home. I just wanted to make sure he was fine." She pulled away. Her gaze went back to the sleeping Trent, and her heart constricted. She wanted to give him a hug and hold him tight.

"He'll be released tomorrow or the day after," Brock said.

"I know." She took a step toward the elevators. Clearly, Brock wasn't ready to stop talking, because he followed her.

"Are you still beating yourself up over not realizing Anthony Holmes was our killer?"

She stopped and looked up at his face. "I should have known he was linked to Derek."

Brock shook his head. "You couldn't have known about sibling rivalry. You weren't raised in a normal household. It was impossible for you to guess."

"I should have realized it when he was in all the photos but then wasn't around."

"How? Magic? He wasn't showing his face in any of the pictures."

"But everyone mentioned how he was always with his brother. I didn't pick up on it when I should have."

"You know this is like putting a puzzle together. We were given clues and we tried to fit the pieces into different slots. Sometimes we figure it out faster than others. It's part of the job. You stopped him. You need to let it go."

She sighed and headed to the elevators.

"Erica…"

"Yes?"

"Give the man a chance," he said after a moment.

She stopped in front of the elevator bank and glanced up into Brock's concerned eyes.

"What are you talking about?" She gulped. Was it that obvious that she had feelings for Trent?

He shrugged. "Trent cares about you."

Did he? He'd said he loved her, but what if he didn't mean it? Maybe that was adrenaline and fear talking, because he thought was going to die. "He cares about all women, Brock."

"If you love him, why not take a chance? Why not give him the benefit of the doubt?" Brock smiled with understanding. "He put his own life at risk for yours. I really think you need to think about that before cutting him off."

How much more did she need to trust him? If she were going to follow her heart, something she'd never done before, then she needed to know he was fully committed too. The way things stood she had no idea what Trent was thinking. They hadn't had a single conversation since he'd been brought home.

"You've made it difficult for him to speak to you. He wakes up sometimes, and when he does, you're all he asks for." Brock sighed in frustration.

She looked up at her long-time friend and finally admitted her biggest concern. "I'm scared. What if he decides I'm too weird for him?"

Brock pulled her into a hug. "I don't think there's any chance of that. You're amazing, and he knows it."

But he hadn't told Erica that. And she needed to hear it from him before she jumped into a pool without knowing how to swim. Relationships were scary things. She had never committed to anyone, so it was weird to think of being committed to someone like Trent. The truth was that underneath all the bullshit, he was a nice guy. And he made her happy. She pulled away from Brock and walked into the elevator.

"I'll see you in a few days." She waved when the door started to shut. Brock nodded and turned back toward the room. Trent was going to be fine, and she needed a break after the last case. Brock had insisted she take vacation. Her time off, away from the aftermath and paperwork, was needed for her mental health.

Two days later, Erica was home, still wearing her pajamas, when her bell rang. She had just finished her first cup of coffee. She opened the door and was immediately grabbed by a pair of hands and hauled into a muscular body.

She gasped. It took nanoseconds for her resistance to melt. A whimper sounded in the back of her throat when he licked and nipped at her lips. His tongue flicked over hers in slow, sensuous waves that pushed her to rub closer to him. Fire erupted in her veins, and all her focus narrowed to just feeling him touch her. His hands gripped her hips and held her in place while the steel of his cock rubbed against her belly. A sliver of logic broke through the sensual haze. Jesus, what the hell was she doing?

Blindly, she stepped back out of his grasp. She needed to put some distance between them.

She cleared her throat and watched him try to catch his breath. The smoldering look he gave her did nothing to help her think. "Trent. How…um, how are you feeling?"

Erica stepped back and away from Trent. His eyes were bright, and his wild side was visible in his tightly drawn features. Her pussy clenched and desire flooded her body.

"I'm feeling like you are trying to hide from me." He took a step toward her.

She blinked at his accusation. "Why would I try to hide from you?"

"I don't know. I tell you I love you, and all of a sudden I never see you again." He took another step toward her.

She tried to focus on his words, but it was hard when he looked so good and she'd missed him so much. All she could think of was licking his jaw and biting his sexy lip. Holy crap. How the hell was she supposed to stay away and work with him while feeling like that?

She folded her arms over her chest. "You love all women, Trent."

"No, I don't. I'm nice to all women. I've never told anyone I love them other than my mother." He was closing the distance between them fast.

Erica, shocked into immobility, almost jumped out of her skin when he grabbed her by her arms. She looked up into his sexy eyes, and warmth spread through her. "You're the first woman I've said I love you to. It would've been a lie to say it before, so I never did. Erica, you're my mate. My mate."

"Trent, I don't know…"

His hand moved up to caress her cheek. "What about your family? You're a shifter! What will they think of you being with a human?"

She gnawed on her lip.

"Once you meet my mom and sisters, you'll see there's nothing to fear. They're amazing. They'll love you. They know you're my mate. You're the woman I love, and that's all that's important to them." He rubbed her arms, soothing her concern. "You might think me a Casanova, but the truth is I have never been out with more than one woman at a time."

He continued to hold her, giving her that soft look that melted the insides of her heart. "My mom always says that just because something didn't work out didn't mean I had to become an insensitive jerk. Besides, my mom and sisters would have my head if I treated any woman poorly. Trust me they're going to love you as much as I love you."

"I've never had a family. What if I mess up? What if I don't fit in?"

"That's what I'm here for, to help you up whenever you fall. Nothing is ever going to be perfect. Take a chance on me, please." His voice was rough and emotional. She wanted to leap away from the fear and into what he was proposing, but she was scared.

"But…but what if you change your mind afterward?" The thought alone made her want to cry.

"You're my mate. Don't you understand what that means? You are the only woman for me and my wolf. There will be no changing my mind. I don't want anyone else. I love you. I know you're unique, and you don't see things like other women." He stopped, lowered his head, and gave her a light kiss on her lips. "But that's what makes you so special, and I wouldn't change that about you for anything in the world."

He stepped away from her, and she wanted to ask him to hold her again.

"You care about these victims more than anyone, because you know how much they suffered. I know you find it hard to trust people. I'm not going to rush you into it. We can take things slowly. But I can't let you go." He stepped in front of her again and cupped her face with his hands. The determination in his gaze turned possessive. "I won't let you go."

The feelings she'd been trying to suppress bubbled up inside her and made her eyes water. She fisted her hands at her sides, hoping to control the need to jump him and hug him to death. He must have seen her emotional turmoil, because his voice lowered to a soothing whisper. "I love *you*, Erica. Only you. No one else but you. Can you love me back?"

She nodded, unable to fight her feelings any longer. "I love you too, Trent." The words came out a watery whisper. Her hands went up around his neck and hugged him close to her.

"Thank god, sweetheart." He pulled back and glanced down at her. "So can you give us a chance? You and me together. No timestamp and no expiration date?" He looked at her straight in the eyes. The love she saw in his eyes made the decision for her.

Her throat closed up but she managed to answer him. "Yes. But know this means you won't be able to date other women. If you do I'll have to kick your ass."

He laughed. "We seriously need to talk about this violence, love. I told you, I only want you."

And then he kissed her with so much tenderness her heart soared. For the first time in her life, she felt someone truly cared. And she wanted to trust him. He'd put her life before his own. He understood she was different and loved her anyway. No one had ever done that.

When he picked her up in his arms, she squealed and pointed him to the bedroom. Now that she had agreed to be his, she wanted to feel his body filling hers again.

"Let's go to bed." He nuzzled her lips. "I want to show you how much I love you."

She sighed, dropped her head into the curve of his shoulder, and smiled as he carried her to her room.

EPILOGUE

Erica lay back in Trent's arms, taking in the sunset and the warm Caribbean air caressing her skin. His lips trailed the back of her ear down to her shoulder. She sighed and turned her face to allow their lips to meet in a hot kiss.

"So what did Brock want?" Trent asked after nibbling on her lips and turning her brain into a useless puddle of goo.

"Hmm?" Her eyes closed as she enjoyed the feel of her new husband's hands sliding up and down her stomach.

He laughed and moved his hands up to cup her breasts over her bikini.

"You are such a tease." She groaned.

"Tell me what Brock wanted, and I can make this so good you'll be screaming my name in seconds. And I know you love screaming my name," he whispered and licked the shell of her ear, making her shiver.

"He wanted to complain about his new boss." She sighed and melted back into him. Her legs widened, allowing one of his hands to dip between her thighs and into her bikini bottom. His fingers spread her pussy lips and massaged her clit. She moaned and rolled her hips on his digits, looking for penetration.

He chuckled. "Uh-uh. What else did he say?"

She growled. "He's not happy… The new team member is a woman he knew…from when he was in college. Apparently they have…uh, unresolved issues."

Trent's hands stopped moving. "What do you mean a woman he knew? As in someone he dated?"

She nodded. "Um hm. Trent, please. I'm dying here."

"I got you baby. You'll be calling me god in about a minute."

She laughed. She was glad she'd taken a chance on the love of her wolf, because he was well worth it.

MILLY TAIDEN

THE END

SIGN UP FOR MILLY'S NEWSLETTER FOR LATEST NEWS!

http://eepurl.com/pt9q1

About the Author

New York Times and USA Today Bestselling Author

Hi! I'm Milly Taiden. I love to write sexy stories featuring fun, sassy heroines with curves and growly alpha males with fur. My books are a great way to satisfy your craving for paranormal romance with action, humor, suspense and happily ever afters.

I live in Florida with my hubby, our boys, and our fur children "Needy Speedy" and "Stormy." Yes, I am aware I'm bossy, and I am seriously addicted to iced caramel lattes.

I love to meet new readers, so come sign up for my

newsletter and check out my Facebook page. We always have lots of fun stuff going on there.

Find out more about Milly Taiden here:

Email: millytaiden@gmail.com

Website: http://www.millytaiden.com

Facebook: http://www.facebook.com/millytaidenpage

Twitter: https://www.twitter.com/millytaiden

If you liked this story, you might also enjoy the following by Milly Taiden:

Sassy Ever After Series

Scent of a Mate *Book One*

A Mate's Bite *Book Two*

Unexpectedly Mated *Book Three*

A Sassy Wedding *Short 3.7*

The Mate Challenge *Book Four*

Sassy in Diapers *Short 4.3*

Fighting for Her Mate *Book Five*

A Fang in the Sass *Book 6*

Shifters Undercover

Bearly in Control *Book One*

Federal Paranormal Unit

Wolf Protector *Federal Paranormal Unit Book One*

Dangerous Protector *Federal Paranormal Unit Book Two*

Unwanted Protector *Federal Paranormal Unit Book Three*

Black Meadow Pack
Sharp Change *Black Meadows Pack Book One*
Caged Heat *Black Meadows Pack Book Two*

Paranormal Dating Agency
Twice the Growl *Book One*
Geek Bearing Gifts *Book Two*
The Purrfect Match *Book Three*
Curves 'Em Right *Book Four*
Tall, Dark and Panther *Book Five*
The Alion King *Book Six*
There's Snow Escape *Book Seven*
Scaling Her Dragon *Book Eight*
In the Roar *Book Nine*
Scrooge Me Hard *Short One*
Bearfoot and Pregnant *Book Ten*
All Kitten Aside *Book Eleven*
Book 12 *(Coming Soon)*

Raging Falls
Miss Taken *Book One*

Miss Matched *Book Two*

Miss Behaved *Book Three (Coming Soon)*

FUR-ocious Lust - Bears

Fur-Bidden *Book One*

Fur-Gotten *Book Two*

Fur-Given Book *Three*

FUR-ocious Lust - Tigers

Stripe-Tease *Book Four*

Stripe-Search *Book Five*

Stripe-Club *Book Six*

Other Works

A Hero's Pride

A Hero Scarred

Wounded Soldiers Set

Wolf Fever

Fate's Wish

Wynter's Captive

Sinfully Naughty Vol. 1

Club Duo Boxed Set

Don't Drink and Hex

Hex Gone Wild

Hex and Kisses

Alpha Owned

Bitten by Night

Seduced by Days

Mated by Night

Taken by Night

Match Made in Hell

Alpha Geek

If you enjoyed the book, please consider leaving a review, even if it's only a line or two; it would make all the difference and would be very much appreciated.

Thank you!

Made in the USA
Coppell, TX
31 January 2020